Catherine

Dedication

This book is dedicated to my children and grandchildren, who have encouraged me to write the trilogy of Catherine, Maggie and Ella, three very strong women who gain their strength through their faith and the love and support they have for each other, just as we do. I love you all.

Catherine by Evonne D. Haley

Prologue

Catherine watched the fog roll in over the city, slowly creeping inward block by block. From the apartment on the thirtieth floor she watched the lights of the lower skyrises disappear, blinking out one by one; the rolling thick grey blanket snuffing them out as it encroached on the city. Backing up a few steps, her gaze focused on the pane of glass, on the woman reflected there. She did not see a pale, shaking, frightened woman, who had just shot the person lying on the carpet six feet behind her. Instead, she saw a strong, determined woman who had just killed someone, who had left her no choice. She turned to make the call.

Catherine by Evonne D. Haley

Chapter 1

(Four months earlier)

Barbara Delong's hand was shaking so badly she could hardly grip her cell phone as she called her friend, Catherine. She would know what to do.

"Hi, Barb," answered Catherine as she saw her caller ID. Before she could say anything else, Barb started crying.

"What's wrong? Are you OK? Barb! Tell me what's going on. Are you home?"

Catherine was really getting concerned. Barbara had problems at home, namely her husband, Ron, who was a cruel man at times. She had urged her to leave him, but things had seemed better lately or Barbara was really putting on a good front. Now things seemed to have come to a head, if she was reading her correctly, listening to her sob.

"Ron's dead!" Barbara gasped out. "On the living room floor. I just found him here.

Catherine by Evonne D. Haley

"OK, I'm on my way. Don't do anything, don't touch anything or speak to anyone until I get there!" Catherine grabbed her keys and coat even as she was running out of her office downtown as she spoke. Eight o'clock at night and she was still working; nothing new.

Twenty minutes later when Catherine arrived, Barbara had stopped crying and was sitting on the couch just staring at nothing. She hadn't even locked the door, Catherine noted as she laid her coat over the briefcase, sat down by Barb on the couch and took her shaking hands in hers.

As she looked around the room, she saw nothing out of place, so there was no struggle here. In fact, the place was so clean, it was sterile, like it was a model home. There was no clutter, no sign that anyone lived here or had ever left a signature of their passing. The living room was huge with floor to ceiling windows overlooking the park across the street; the entire townhouse was at least three thousand square feet. The decor was modern with lots of glass and chrome, some very nice artwork on the walls. Catherine felt it was cold, unlived in.

"OK, tell me what happened," she encouraged Barbara as she finally looked at the body on the floor. He was lying on the floor with his hands folded on his chest, like a corpse laid out in a coffin. His suit was Armani, his tie silk.

"I just came home from work and he was lying there on the floor. Dead."

"How did you know he was dead? Did you touch him?" probed Catherine.

"No. He was just dead. I could tell." Barbara was starting to come out of it as Catherine rubbed her back and encouraged her to speak.

"Did you tell anyone, other than me? Did you call 911?"

"No. Just you, Catherine. I knew you would know what to do."

"Good. OK. Did you and Ron have a fight? Did he hurt you?" Catherine was looking at Barbara, searching for bruises.

"No! I told you. I just came home from work and found him dead on the floor! Don't you believe me?" Barbara was getting agitated.

"Yes. I do. I am calling someone who will help us deal with this. Ok? I will stay with you as your lawyer and help you through this."

"Thank you, Catherine," Barbara nodded as she clasped her hands.

Catherine dialed her boss and told him the details of the events. He would call the police chief and get the ball rolling.

Chapter 2

Detective Jeremy Slade entered the Delong's townhouse after signing in with the police crime scene recorder and donning the blue booties and latex gloves required at a crime scene. He stood in the entryway and examined the room. The technicians were dusting for fingerprints and taking pictures of the scene. The room was busy. He went over to the body, which was being photographed and examined by the medical examiner, Patricia O'Donnell. She was a mature woman of fifty-six years, slightly heavy with discerning eyes and the reputation of being the best in her field.

"So, Pat. Anything you can tell me about our victim?" Slade asked.

"Well, it has to be the neatest corpse I've ever seen. Looks like he was brought here and posed like he was already in the casket. Arms were folded with his hands clasped together on his chest. I think they even combed his hair. Weird. From the lividity and liver temperature,

I can say he died somewhere else around seven to seven-thirty p.m. today and was then brought here. Cause of death appears to be a bullet to the heart, close range, possibly a 9 milometer. I will give you a more complete report after I do the autopsy. We are finished here. Ready to roll, guys." The ME and her team wheeled the body in the black body bag out on the gurney.

Slade went over to the crime scene lead technician, a tall bald man, who was known for enforcing his exact guidelines at the crime scene and in forensic analysis.

"Anything stand out to you, Stan?" he asked.

"He bled out somewhere else. Hardly any blood here at all. Reminds me of a case in '82, a mob hit with the same funeral pose. It turned out to be a warning to another crime family. Also, this has to be the cleanest and neatest crime scene I have ever seen. I will know more when the forensic test results come in."

9

"I was told the wife found him. Where is she?" inquired Slade. "Was she tested for gunshot residue?"

"She is in the bedroom with Constable White and her lawyer," replied Stan, "and she was negative for GSR on her hands or clothes, which was weird, but then she said she didn't touch him."

At Slade's raised eyebrow, Stan said, "Yeah, I thought that, too. What wife wouldn't touch her husband to see if he was still alive. But she is too small to have moved a man his size without help. Oh well, that is your job, isn't it, to find the who and why?"

With that consideration, Slade headed for the bedroom to meet Mrs. Delong and her lawyer. The lawyer interested him, because she was the one who called someone who called his boss, the Chief of Police, who called him as Senior Homicide Detective with instructions on how he was to treat the wife of the victim. Carefully and gently were his instructions.

Catherine by Evonne D. Haley

From the doorway, Slade observed the three women in the room. He nodded to Constable White and she left the room. The other two women were packing a suitcase. He identified the lawyer right away. She was concerned and considerate with Barbara Delong encouraging her to pack the clothes she would need while the townhouse was quarantined as a crime scene.

Barbara Delong was a petite brunette about five feet four inches tall, slim, beautiful brown eyes, sable hair worn in a bob to her shoulders, all in all a lovely woman. She seemed to be subdued, or it could be that she was in shock from finding her dead husband.

Her lawyer, Catherine Henley, was in charge. She spoke to Barbara, gently coordinating her movements. She was tiny, not just petite at five-foot three inches, but tiny as well. People who took that look as being weak would be very surprised. Slade had done a quick search on her. He wanted to know who could make one phone call that caused his boss to tell him how to run his investigation. What he found was that Catherine was a very strong woman who had put herself through law school working three jobs after her husband had left her while she was pregnant. The child had been stillborn.

From there she focused totally on her career. With an honor's in International Law, she had joined a well-known law firm and rose quickly up the ranks. After seeing her beautiful blue eyes and calm, gentle manner with Barbara, Slade realized that her ex-husband was an idiot. Most men would want to look after her, rescue her, but she didn't need that. She was a power house on her own. Her slight appearance didn't reflect the intelligence behind those baby blues, her strength, or even her ability to play a song on the piano after hearing the song just once, as he would find out later. She was truly an enigma. One he might like to get to know a little better.

"Hello, ladies," he spoke from the doorway of the bedroom. "May I ask you a few questions, Mrs. Delong?"

Catherine turned and looked at him. He was tall, six-foot three at least and muscular with slightly long dark hair that reached his collar and striking blue eyes. Maybe a former college football player who had stayed in shape after college; no, she reconsidered, an ex-marine. He had the eyes of a soldier who had seen more than he should and more than he could forget, but he also had a hint of amusement in his expression that was out of line with the situation, as if he could see the humor with life in all its vistas. She could also see interest in his eyes as he stared at her.

"You are?" she asked.

"Detective Jeremy Slade, TOPD, Homicide Division. And you are?" he asked in kind, but he kept his voice soft.

"I am Catherine Henley, Barbara's friend and lawyer. Please keep your questions brief. She needs to see a doctor for shock and to get some rest. She will be available tomorrow for a full debriefing." Catherine was really concerned for her friend as she was getting

13

quieter and barely able to make a decision on what to pack.

"I'm glad to see she has such a close friend as her lawyer. These situations can be very stressful. Let's sit over here shall we?" Slade motioned them both to the seating arrangement of a love seat and two club chairs in front of a gas fire that was burning. It was a sumptuous bedroom, with comfort in mind, a place to relax, private.

"Barb was cold," Catherine told him when he looked at the fire that was enclosed behind glass and he nodded. The crime scene technicians had already cleared the room before Mrs. Delong was allowed in to get her personal items and clothing under the scrutiny of the female police officer.

"Now, Mrs. Delong. Can you trace your steps this evening for me? Just tell me what you did from around four this afternoon up to now." The detective spoke softly, keeping his voice calm and encouraging.

"I was at work all day at our firm Carter & Delong at 1040 Richmond Street East. I had meetings all day long until six o`clock. I left the office around 6:30, but I didn't get home until 7:45, because there was an accident at Young and Bloor and traffic was tied up for over an hour. When I got here I found Max here on the step with her leash on, shaking with cold." Barbara stroked the miniature Yorkshire terrier on her lap as she spoke. It couldn't have weighed three pounds and certainly wasn't a guard dog. How would a person walk such a small dog without dragging it along? But, it was very cute. Every few seconds it would shake from head to toe. Barbara's gentle strokes calmed her down. You could see it was traumatized.

"Then I came in and found Ron on the floor. He was dead." Barb's voice was breaking at the end of her speech.

Well, that was certainly concise enough; well rehearsed Slade thought. Had the lawyer gone over her statement with her?

Catherine by Evonne D. Haley

"Do you know where your husband was today? What was his routine?"

" He was at the office all day and then he had a meeting at 3:30 this afternoon with clients outside the office."

"You work together?"

"Yes," she confirmed.

"I will need their contact information," Slade told her." Did you speak to him after he left the office?"

"No, I was in meetings until six like I said." she answered as she frowned at him.

"Did you touch him?"

"What?" she seemed confused.

"Did you touch your husband when you found him on the floor?" he repeated and watched her closely as she struggled for an answer.

"No, I could tell he wasn't breathing." Barbara was shaking as she patted Max.

"Then what happened?"

Catherine by Evonne D. Haley

"What happened?" She seemed confused.

"Did you call 911 or the police?" he asked watching her eyes. This seemed to be the point where she was uncertain.

"No," she said.

"No?"

"No. I called Catherine. I knew she would know what to do."

Slade watched as she looked to her friend for what? Encouragement? Answers?

"Then what happened?" he asked again.

"Catherine came and called someone and the police came. That's it. That's what happened."

"Ok, that's enough for now." He could tell she was barely coherent. "You may leave and go to your lawyer's house. We can have a more formal interview tomorrow and you can give us your written statement then. Just give me your address and contact numbers so I may reach you if I have more questions." He looked at Catherine as he spoke. She quirked

17

an eyebrow at him and passed him her business card that had the information he needed as well as her home and cell numbers already written on the back. This was one put together lady Slade thought as Catherine ushered Barbara out the door picking up her coat and briefcase as they left.

Chapter 3

Two days later Slade arrived at the offices of Carter & Delong at nine in the morning. The receptionist was red-eyed but professional as she asked if she could help him. She was a voluptuous blond wearing a tight black sweater. She would definitely stop traffic.

"Yes. I am Detective Slade of the Toronto police. I am investigating the death of Mr. Delong. Is there someone I can speak with besides Mrs. Delong? I assume she's not here today," he asked politely.

"Yes, Mrs. Delong is here in her office. Just a moment and I will see if she can see you," the girl replied as she pressed a key and said, "Detective Slade is here to see you," she announced. She listened in her ear set and then said, "She will see you. Please follow me."

"What is your name, Miss?" Slade asked as he followed her down a hall to the right of her desk.

"I am Jean Jones, but everyone calls me J.J." She smiled at him over her shoulder as she led him all the way to the end of the corridor and knocked on the door that said Barbara Delong, President and CEO. Slade looked across the hall to the opposite door that was closed entitled Ron Delong, Director of Account Management and Sales. That was telling, thought Slade, a nice title that didn't give him any power. J.J. knocked and opened the door as Barbara said, "Enter."

Inside, her corner office was impressively large with a brown leather couch, club chairs and a glass coffee table arranged to the left side of the door. To the right side of the door there was a conference table with blue leather swivel arm chairs to seat eight. Barbara's desk was solid mahogany, a beautiful piece of furniture in front of floor to ceiling windows on both sides of the corner office. The solid wall on the left held a built-in bar with glasses and a sink with a fridge.

"Would you like a coffee, tea or water, Detective Slade?" Barbara offered.

"Coffee would be great," he replied. "Two sugars and cream, please," and he smiled at J.J. as she hurried to get it. Barbara already had a cup on her desk.

"Thank you for coming to the station this morning with your lawyer and giving your formal statement. Mrs. Henley must be a great comfort to you right now. I am sorry to bother you at work, but I have a few more questions. I am surprised to see you here at the office." Slade accepted the cup of coffee J.J. passed him as he seated himself in the blue club chair in front of her desk.

"Thank you, J.J." Barb said dismissing her.

"I needed to keep busy and since I couldn't go home, I came to work. My daughters are flying in tonight, so I will be with them after today. What can I do for you, Detective?"

She seemed much calmer today, not in shock and quite in charge in her work environment. She was dressed in a black silk suit and red silk blouse that probably cost more that his monthly salary. Her makeup was subtle, and she had tried to cover the dark circles under her eyes, almost succeeding. She had probably not slept much the last few nights.

"Did your husband have any enemies? Has he ever been threatened or received any hate mail?" Slade watched her face carefully as he asked the questions.

"Not that I know. We are financial consultants. Most of our clients are old money with trust accounts that we monitor, and we oversee their investments. Not very exciting, I'm afraid." She smiled slightly, despairingly.

"You said your husband left the office around three that afternoon. Was he walking, taking a cab or driving his car?"

"His car was getting detailed, so he was walking that day, which wasn't unusual. It's so hard to find parking downtown; he always said he could walk faster."

"Where was his appointment? Do you know who he was meeting with that day?" Slade was asking a question after a question.

This method often caused people to answer without thinking, giving away more than they wanted. However, he didn't believe Barb was trying to be deceitful.

"His meeting was downtown, that's all I know, but J.J. should have those details. She can give you the information at the front desk," Barbara answered.

"OK, that's it for now, unless you have something to say or do you have any concerns?" Slade was watching her eyes. He had already verified her timeline after she left her office until she arrived home. There had been an accident downtown that tied up traffic for over an hour.

"Not that I can think of right now. I need to make funeral arrangements. When...when do I get the..." she couldn't say `body`.

"That's up to the medical examiner, but I will find out for you." Slade was using kid gloves as he was commanded even though the spouse was the first person to be suspected in a homicide of this kind. She had cooperated with the GSR test, which was negative for gunshot residue. That, in itself, was interesting. Very interesting. What wife would find her husband lying on the floor and not touch him to see if he was hurt, or still alive or even to make sure he was dead, if he looked like he was?

And then to call her friendly lawyer instead of 911? Really strange; and yet, he didn't think she did it. The positioning of the body in their home was definitely a message, a warning; but to whom? The wife would be the obvious answer; but more importantly, what was the message? Slade now had to find the real crime scene so he would follow the victim's steps after he left his office to see where that led him.

Chapter 4

Catherine stared at her boss, at a loss for words. He had just told her to stay clear of the investigation into Ron's death.

"The Toronto Police Department has a good detective on it, so let him do his job. I want you to focus on your current case; find out where the money is coming from to support the terrorist cell and confirm what their target is. Keep me updated. Dismissed."

Director Robert Blanchette had a stressful job, which he excelled at. He could departmentalize and delegate while keeping abreast of cases and their investigators. He was always there to support and back up his people, but he also didn't allow them to become overloaded with the pressure of keeping ahead of terrorist threats to their homeland. It was now a fact of life that they all had to cope with, which meant their jobs were a marathon and not normally a sprint. Their innocence of the evil in the world was gone. Canada was the best country in the world to live in and their jobs were to keep it so.

Her office on Queen Street looked like a regular lawyer's office, and although she was a lawyer, her real job was with CSIS, Canadian Security Intelligence Services, equivalent to the US's CIA and Britain's MI6, where she analyzed activities suspected of constituting threats to the security of Canada, including terrorism and espionage. She worked in direct affiliation with the Department of Justice and the Financial Transactions and Reports Analysis Center of Canada, specifically, regarding money laundering and terrorist financing.

One of her top cases right now focused on a terrorist group believed to be in Canada right in her own city. The information was sketchy, but they were following the finances of a non-profit organization requesting money for Syrian refugees. The person they knew was involved was an Iranian named Sameer. From the e-mails and cell phone intercepts, he was dealing with a known arms dealer in Iran, who also appeared to be a cousin or relative of some kind. The intercepts were discussions concerning their uncle's failing health. The CSIS was focused on this case, as they believed there was a threat of attack in Toronto, a city of over four million people. Catherine and her team were working solely on this case when everything changed. The intercepts became angry and abrupt. The message was that the uncle was in a coma and they couldn't pay the hospital bill. Something had interrupted the flow of money involving a third party, possibly a coup of some kind. It was her job to find out what and to follow the money.

Catherine left her boss's office with her mind racing. She would have to call Barbara to see if she was OK and whether she needed help with the funeral arrangements. Catherine wouldn't be working the case, but she would be there for her friend. She couldn't be actively involved in the investigation, but she could stay abreast of it. She would be there for Barb if she needed her.

Chapter 5

Maggie O'Donnell walked across the restaurant to the table by the window, where Ella Lewis was waiting for her and Catherine to have lunch. Ella watched her move toward her and smiled. Every man in the restaurant watched Maggie cross the room. At five feet four inches with blonde hair and striking blue eyes plus porcelain skin she was beautiful, but there was also a charisma about her that drew men to her like a moth to a flame. Ella didn't know what it was, but she had seen it happen many times. Maggie could wear a red hoodie, purple shorts and orange leg warmers and still get hit on jogging in the park. Seriously, that had happened.

Maggie smiled at Ella, totally unaware of the effect she was causing. She was watching the petite brunette with beautiful hazel eyes grin at her from across the room. Ella had a mischievous air about her, like a pixie with a secret. She also had had her share of male attention, but she rarely reciprocated or answered that call. Like Maggie she had a full life. She was an English professor at the University of Toronto, a published author, mother of two daughters and one grown son she had raised alone since the divorce, and a great friend.

Maggie also had raised a grown son whom she adored. Her husband had died in an auto accident shortly before his birth. As the owner of a real estate agency based in Toronto, her hours were long and she worked on the whim of buyers and sellers. But her son had always come first. She made sure he was grounded and had his interests explored and developed, especially his music. She had fronted his music production studio at first, but now he was doing well on his own. She was very proud of him.

Two very busy women, independent, successful, and strong. They were strong because life had forced it on them. Had beat at them until they had to strike back or give up, give in to life and fail, but never as mothers, and never as friends. Their friendship was the force that enabled them to win, that

29

held them up when everything in their lives was trying to beat them down. They even had a name for it, for the days where they might have given in except for that friendship. They called it the 'break the bottle' days.

Ella remembered the first time it happened to her. When her girls were in high school, she was shopping for groceries late on a Friday night after a really trying week, several weeks actually. It was the first chance she had had and she was tired, extremely tired. She hadn't made her grocery list; so, in every aisle, she had at least twenty decisions to make. Should she get pasta? Didn't she have pasta at home or did she use it all for dinner the other night? What about sauce? Which kind should she get, with garlic or without? Pickles, her daughter, Tanya, liked dill pickles and beets. Ella grabbed a bottle of beets, but it slipped through her fingers and crashed on the floor. Little round purple beets rolled up the aisle making strange squiggly, purple marks in every direction.

Ella just stood there, watching the mess unfold. She started trembling. Who was going to clean this up?

The stock boy who was filling some bottom shelves, looked up at her from his position squatting on the floor. He was a nice boy and when he saw her face begin to crumble, he jumped up and said, "It's OK. I'll clean it up. No worries."

He knew she was going to lose it and cry. He hated it when his mother cried, so he would try to keep this lady from crying, too.

Ella looked at him and then down at the purple mess on the floor. She just shut down, left the half full grocery cart, walked out of the store, somehow made her way home, collapsed on her bed and cried. Her daughters, Tanya and Roberta, who were in the family room watching a movie, looked at each other. What happened? Their mother never cried. What were they supposed to do? She didn't respond to their worried queries as they knocked on her door, which frightened them even more. So, they called Maggie. She would know what to do.

Maggie arrived within twenty minutes. She hugged the girls, reassured them all would be well, went into the bedroom closing the door and sat on the bed beside Ella and rubbed her back.

"What's the matter, honey? What's going on? Had a rough day?" She tried to bring her out of sobbing into the pillow.

Finally, Ella calmed enough to try to talk. "I just couldn't take it anymore. Just one more decision to make, one more mess to clean up. All those purple beets rolling down the aisle! And I am so tired!"

"Okay," drawled Maggie. "I hope that means you were grocery shopping. Otherwise the beet thing would be really weird!" She kept rubbing Ella's back. "Why were you doing that on a Friday night at nearly midnight?"

"It was the only time I had left. It has been so busy at work, the girls are into every sport going, so I have to take them to their practices and games and I have been doing paperwork in the observation deck at the stadium while trying not to miss their goals..." She broke off with a sob.

"So that is why you missed lunch with Catherine and I last Wednesday. Ok, we must time manage you better. You need to learn to say 'no' and decide what is most important in your life. Yes, your job is important, but so are you. Your life is important or you're doing all this for nothing. Andrew is out on his own, thriving in his field as an anthropologist. The girls are older now. They can learn to do some of the things you do, like the laundry, cooking, even getting the groceries. You need to let go of some of your responsibilities. Tanya has her license, so she can drive them to the practices, and you can go to the games."

"Yes, Mom. We can do that and help more at home. Don't cry, Mom. We love you." Both girls came in from the hallway where they were listening and hugged their mother.

"I love you both, girls. I'm sorry for making a scene. I was overwhelmed with everything. It wasn't just you, it was too much of my life hitting me and I am tired, physically as well as mentally." Ella tried to explain it to her daughters. She didn't want them to feel bad, like it was all their fault. Yes, they could help out more at home, take responsibility for cleaning up after themselves, doing their own laundry, but a lot of her stress, besides her job, was because she didn't have time to herself. She had no 'me' time. And no more missing lunch with the girlfriends. Maggie and Catherine were her "life lines" and her "laugh lines." She needed that time with them, so she would not have 'break the bottle' days like this. Thank God for them. But then maybe meltdowns occasionally were good if they made positive changes. Who knew?

"What's with the grin? What did you do now?" asked Maggie as she sat down at the table.

"Just thinking of the 'break the bottle' beet fiasco and how much I appreciate you and

34

Catherine." Ella replied. "Where is Catherine? Isn't she coming?"

"There she is," Maggie waved to her as she came into the restaurant.

Catherine waved back, moving toward them. She was the calm, quiet one of the threesome in public. When there was just the three of them, she could let down her hair and be surprisingly funny. She had a droll sense of humor. They were, all three, so close to each other, they trusted each other implicitly; and they loved each other more than sisters, more than friends. They relied on each other and they never failed each other. They had made a pact twenty years before to always be there for each other through husbands, children, jobs, divorce, whatever life threw at them.

Now that Maggie and Ella's children were practically all grown up, they were all moving into a different side of life. Letting go of the joy of motherhood and moving into the joy of watching their children become self-reliant adults was very hard for some mothers.

Maggie hem through this part of their lives. Ella's girls were both in college now, Maggie's son was doing very well with his music business, and Catherine was mother to all of them. Not having children, herself, gave her a different viewpoint that was appreciated by Maggie and Ella, one not so emotionally charged at times. They each brought something different to their friendship.

As soon as the 'hellos' and kisses and hugs were all done, Catherine said, "We have a problem. Barbara's husband, Ron, was murdered and left in their apartment. She is suspect number one at this point."

She told them as much as she could of what had transpired without revealing what was not available to the public.

Ella and Maggie both gasped and said together, "Is she OK?"

Although Barbara was closer to Catherine, she was a friend to all three of them.

"She's staying at my place for a few days, because her apartment is closed off as the crime scene. She wants me to be her lawyer, but I am turning her case over to one of my friends, who has more experience as a criminal lawyer."

Ella and Maggie both knew what Catherine really did for the CSIS.

Catherine continued, "Barb has an alibi for the time of death, but she could have had someone else do it for her." She put her hand up to stop their immediate denial of that happening. "That is just what I am getting from the lead detective."

"Well, I know we have all thought of killing him, but none of us did." She paused. "Right?" Ella asked.

The three of them looked at each other and broke out laughing simultaneously.

"Right!" They all agreed.

"He has been in some shady deals and played with other people's money, even losing some, so the police will have lots of suspects to investigate," said Maggie.

"But it was the way the body was found that gives me a really bad feeling. He was killed someplace else and then moved to Barb's townhouse. He was laid out on the floor with his arms folded on his chest with his fingers clasped, like he would have been in a casket." Catherine shivered.

"Why? What would be the purpose of doing that?" asked Ella. "Were they trying to implicate Barbara? Make it look like she had done it?"

"No. There was hardly any blood at the scene, so the police knew he was killed somewhere else and Barb is too small to move a dead body. Besides, she wouldn't have moved it to her own house implicating herself. No. There is something else going on here. I think if they find out why his body was moved there, they will find out why he was killed."

"Ok, what can we do for Barb?" asked Maggie.

"She can continue staying at my place now that I am not her lawyer, but why don't you both come over tonight and we will try to get her to relax a little. Just to let her know she isn't alone and we are there for her. Ok?"

Ella and Maggie nodded, "Sure, we will be there. I'll bring wine," said Maggie.

"I'll bring lasagna," said Ella. "I made it late last night, but the girls can order in. They'll like that better anyway."

"Ok, great. I love your lasagna! I'll pick up a salad and garlic bread. We'll have a feast." Catherine smiled at her two closest friends. "You are always there for me. Thank you."

Chapter 6

Detective Slade was looking through the case file of the hit that the crime scene tech, Stan, had told him about. It was the positioning of the body that bothered Slade. If this was a warning, who was being warned? The wife, Barbara? She seemed the most obvious person. It was her home, her husband, so it seemed clear she was being warned, but of what? And why? Was it personal or professional? They did look after a lot of money, other people's money. Could the victim have embezzled money from one of their clients? Slade would need a warrant to have financial forensics go through the company's accounts, but he didn't have enough justifiable cause yet to get that warrant. The Delong's clients were very wealthy and knew all the city's political players. They would have a problem with people going through their accounts.

His cell phone rang, "Slade here," he answered and listened to the caller.

"I'm on my way." They had found the original crime scene.

Slade arrived at Cottingham Street where it turned into Orange Street just across the park from the Delong's condo on Birch Street. There were trees and bushes to hide a body in, plus the railway tracks ran parallel to Cottingham, which could have muffled any shots fired when the train went by. So why move it? It kept coming back to why he was posed in the townhouse.

"So, Stan, how are you doing? Anything stand out? Who found the body?" Slade greeted the crime scene technician.

"The guy over there by Coleson, who is taking his statement, was walking his dog and noticed where the blood had run down the sidewalk. His dog got it on his paws and muzzle. If it's Delong's, he definitely bled out here. There is a lot of blood. I'll know more when we have processed the complete scene and have the reports back from the lab."

"Thanks, Stan," Slade walked away from the crime scene across the street to the park and looked directly at the Delong's townhouse on Birch Street. They could have carried the body across the park, but that would be really ballsy, too many chances of being seen. He would come back after dark to see what went on in this park from six-thirty to seven-thirty, the coroner's estimated time of death, to see the normal activities of the neighborhood.

Chapter 7

Catherine finished setting the table just as the doorbell rang.

"Hello, ladies," she greeted Ella and Maggie at the door. "Give me your coats and go on in. Barb is in the living room."

"Hello, honey," Ella greeted Barb with a hug. "How are you doing? You know we are here for you, don't you? You just have to let us know what you need. Ok?"

Maggie hugged Barb as well. "Whatever and wherever at any time, honey," Maggie remembered what it was like to get through her husband's funeral.

"Thank you both, so much. I just don't know what I need at this point. I have to get through the funeral details, but they won't release his body....," Barb stumbled to a stop.

"The medical examiner should do that soon, Barb, but we can help you get through this. You are not alone," Catherine encouraged her. "We know how disorienting it is to make

43

all these decisions when you are under so much stress. We will be with you every step of the way, until you don't need us or don't want us there."

"You don't know how much I appreciate this," Barb said with tears in her eyes. "You have all been so great." She finished on a soft little sob.

"Ok, that`s settled. Who wants red wine or white?" offered Catherine.

"I`ll have Chardonnay, please," said Ella.

"Red for me," stated Maggie as she settled on the couch by Barb.

"Me, too," agreed Barb feeling better knowing she had the support of her friends with her, that she wasn't alone.

Tiny little footsteps clicked down the hall to the living room.

"There you are, Max. Come see me," urged Ella. "You are just the cutest little munchkin. Are you limping?" Ella's concerned voice asked as she picked up the miniature Yorkshire Terrier.

"She has a sore leg. I took her to the vet today. He says she'll be OK. It must have happened the other night when she got out. She was on the doorstep when I got home the night I found Ron. She had her leash on, which was really odd, because, as you know, Ron hated her and would never have walked her."

Catherine watched as the girls fussed over the little pooch, thinking. She would call Detective Slade and give him this information. It could mean nothing, but it was odd, nevertheless.

Chapter 8

Slade walked the perimeter of the park from the crime scene to the Delong's town house at six-thirty that night. It was dark before six at this time of year. Some activity, but not crowded and the lighting was low due to several street lights that were out, possibly shot out by Ron Delong's murderers, who they believed had used a silencer on the gun that killed him. There had to be at least two people involved in the murder to move the body without being seen.

There were a lot of trees and shrubs, which shrouded anyone in those areas, especially at the scene where Delong was killed. It was also at the end of a dead-end street and the murder occurred behind the fence in the bushes. Why was he there? It was so close to the townhouse. Was he lured there? It was a strange place for a meeting. Then he noticed a young woman in the park walking her dog.

That was what he must have been doing, walking that little dog of theirs. Mrs. Delong had mentioned she found her on the step. He would talk with her again in the morning. The Delong's also had a courtyard in the front of their place. It was nice, shaded with plenty of trees and a hedge ran all the way around except for the cast iron gate off the driveway, which went under the building to their parking garage. With a little luck, you could get a body out of a car backed up to the gate without anyone seeing. It was dark enough and you would only be visible for maybe twenty to thirty seconds. Two men could do it.

Ok, Slade thought, so Delong takes his little pooch for a walk when he gets home. He would have to determine the time line from Delong's last appointment to when he arrived home. He gets killed on the other side of the park, shoved into a trunk, driven back to the townhouse, carried in and posed on the living room floor. The pooch is left outside, because it ran away when the shooting occurred, probably. Yeah, that could be how it was done. He would check with Stan to see if there were any noticeable tire tracks in the morning. Now to find the 'why'.

Early next morning Catherine Henley walked into the Bloor Street police station and asked for Detective Slade. She was then escorted to his office.

"Good morning, Detective," she greeted him from his doorway.

Catherine was dressed for work in a red suit from Vera Wang's collection. No skin from her neck to her knees was showing, but the way it draped her tiny frame and moved when she did was sensual even while it was professional. Slade smiled at her. She was a contradiction in appearances. She was so petite and feminine, he automatically wanted to protect her. She was also beautiful so he probably should protect her from himself. Yeah, he would like to have a chance.

"Coffee?" he offered.

"Thanks," she accepted his offer. "Black, please."

"Have a seat. What can I do for you?"

"It's what I can do for you. I took this by mistake when I left Barb's that night. It's such a habit to carry my briefcase and when I arrived I had laid my coat on top of it. I didn't look at it until this morning and realized it was Ron's, so I brought it over to you on my way to work. Sorry," Catherine explained the mix up to him rather sheepishly.

"Thanks," she accepted the coffee he had poured for her. "Secondly, I think Ron was walking Max, their little dog, when he was killed. Barb found her on the doorstep when she got home that night and Max was also hurt."

"Maybe she got out when they brought Ron into the house," Slade played devil's advocate.

"No, she had her leash on, otherwise I'd agree with that thought. He must have taken her out when he got home, and somehow, she got away. But that is what is so weird. Ron

49

hated her and wouldn't have taken her out. She always hid in Barb's room when he came home." Catherine was watching him. "You don't seem surprised."

"No, I figured that out last night. We found the original murder scene on the other side of the park across from their townhouse. I also think he was put in the trunk of a car, driven to their place and left there. The `why` I don't know yet. Is Mrs. Delong still staying with you?"

"Yes, I referred her to a colleague in case she needs a lawyer to help her through this; but she needs a friend more, so she will stay with me for a while. You can reach her there. She also wants to get through with the funeral. When do you think the body will be released?"

"A few more days, I suspect," Slade replied. He paused, looking straight at her. "Does your friend have any ideas about who could have killed her husband?"

"Besides her you mean?" she came back at him. "No, she says she doesn't."

50

"Well, that`s telling, isn't it?" he smiled.

"What do you mean?" Catherine wasn't smiling now and she wasn't looking at him either. She knew she had slipped up.

"Do you think she knows why someone would want to kill him or does she know who could have killed him?" Slade asked her point blank.

"Can I be honest with you?"

When he nodded, she continued, "The thing is there are a lot of people who hated him. He wasn't a nice man. The list would be smaller if you asked who didn't want to kill him. Even I wouldn't be on that list. He was a liar, a cheat, a bully and a woman beater. And no, I don't think Barb killed him, though she had every reason to do it. She's not built that way and she loved him. I don't know why, but she did."

Catherine stood up to leave, picking up her coat.

"Well, thanks for coming in with the information about the dog and bringing in the briefcase. I appreciate it," he smiled at her as he stood up and helped her put her coat on.

"You're welcome. Oh, and by the way, the vet said someone kicked Max or stepped on her so you can look for a dog hater." She smiled at him, "Who else would hurt that sweet little Yorkie?"

As Slade watched her leave his office, he suddenly felt afraid for her. The innocent little dog probably got in the way and someone lashed out at her. He didn't want anyone to lash out and hurt the enchanting woman who just left his office. He also doubted her story about the briefcase and that worried him. The people who killed Delong would not hesitate to eliminate her if she got in their way.

As Catherine got in the elevator her thoughts were on the handsome detective she had just left. She was attracted to him; she would have to keep her guard up around him and not let things slip like, "She says she doesn't." He picked up on that immediately and until she had more evidence, she would protect her friend.

Chapter 9

Catherine's team was gathered in the conference room when she arrived at work.

"OK, Craig, what do we have so far on Sameer and his terrorist cell?"

"We believe that he has set up several websites for humanitarian aid. The most active one was called the Syrian Way. We have heard chatter from intercepts that includes this site as a major syphon for funds. The website is set up to receive donations through advertising on social media like Facebook, Twitter, etc. They collect the money through online banking, PayPal, and Bitcoin and within three months they close the site. Their bank accounts are all closed at the same time; they are gone, ghosts. Whoever is setting this all up must know international law for NPOs and banking. So, it seems reasonable that we could be looking for a lawyer or an accountant."

"I need to speak to you, in private," he stood up and headed out the door.

"Ok, what's going on?" she asked him quietly in the hall.

"I went through Delong's computer files like you asked me to last night. The website, Syrian Way, that we believe is a front for Sameer's terrorist cell here in Toronto?"

"Yes, the one we suspect Sameer is using to fund a hit here in Canada. What about it?" she asked.

"It's all through Delong's computer files. I have broken through three firewalls and accessed the files; and while everything looked legal and above board, I dug deeper and found another layer of files. Those were harder to access, impossible for most people, but not for someone with my skills. These files show that the Syrian Way received major funding through Delong's legitimate clients and I don't think they know it."

"Wow! I was not expecting that. Delong was working for Sameer? And what do you mean, Craig? They would know what they were spending their money on."

"Not necessarily. It looks like Delong established this site for humanitarian aid, which is where the firm's clients were donating funds for write offs on their income tax, only at the end of February when there will be no income tax receipts. And there is more. The second set of hidden files shows the complete series of transfers from the one main account to overseas accounts, seven banks in all. From there the money disappears. The reason for the second set of files could only be for blackmail purposes. Normally, this careful and explicit record of following the money would be suicide for whoever was doing it if they got caught. The whole exercise of transferring the money so many times is to lose the trail of the money as they will only give out the destination of those transfers to the owner of the accounts. Plus, to have knowledge of these exact transactions, could only be acquired by the person who made them. That could only be from someone with power of attorney to actually move the money or someone who had authority on the accounts themselves. I am trying to access the names of the trustees of the accounts, but it will take time as I only have account numbers and not the banks or names."

"Well, that is more than I thought we would have at this point. Great work, Craig!"

"There is another layer behind a firewall that I haven't gotten into yet. I will send you a report on what I have so far, but it definitely looks like Delong was into some serious illegal activity."

"Thanks, Craig. I appreciate you doing this in addition to your regular duties. It also breaks open the Sameer case." Catherine made her way to her office and poured a cup of coffee for herself. She stood looking out her window to downtown Toronto. It was such a bustling city, infested with so many people and cars. She wondered how long she had before she would have to give this information to Detective Slade. He had the computer so maybe she didn't have to tell him anything. He could get the same information she had uncovered. She would wait until Craig opened all the files.

Chapter 10

Ten days later, Barbara stood by the casket at the front of the funeral home waiting for the service to start. People were still coming in to pay their respects to her. She stood in her plain black dress and pumps shaking hands, kissing cheeks, and thanking people for their solicitations. She had a faint smile plastered on her face and it felt like it was going to crack with the effort it took to keep it there.

Finally, the last man in the line took her hand. He looked like a successful business man. He wasn't a tall man, a few inches under six feet, but broad, with muscles, dark hair and skin. He would have been handsome, but his eyes were cold and his demeanor was intimidating. He was dressed in a five-thousand-dollar Armani suit, white oxford shirt and a silk tie. He leaned in toward her. She thought he was going to kiss her cheek, but instead he spoke, "Did you get my message?"

"Excuse me, your message?" Barbara said confusedly. "I'm sorry, I don't know what you

59

mean. Did you leave a message with the funeral director?"

"No," he replied still holding her hand. "The message on the floor of your living room."

Barb gasped and tried to pull her hand from his grasp. "Don't react, Mrs. Delong. Smile. I will contact you and we will discuss our problem together. All I want is the money." He let go of her hand. "By the way, you have two very lovely young daughters. Almost as lovely as their mother." He walked away.

Barb watched him go, feeling shaken. What money? What had Ron been into? Was he threatening her girls?

The funeral director went to the podium and asked everyone to take their seats. Barb sat in the front row with her daughters. She just had to make it through the next hour and then she could go home. She had such a headache.

Catherine, Ella and Maggie sat in the row behind her with their families. Catherine

60

leaned forward and patted Barb's shoulder to let her know she wasn't alone. They were there for her. How she made the right responses, Barb didn't know, but she made it through the service and the reception afterwards. Thankfully, Catherine, Ella and Maggie took over, got her through the event and were comforting to her daughters as well.

Ella put her arm around Barb's waist. "I know this is hard, Barb. We can get everyone out of here in fifteen minutes. If you want to take the girls home, go ahead. We will finish up here. There are only a few people left."

"Ok, I have such a headache, I will take you up on that. Thanks so much. I don't know what I would have done without you guys this past week." Barb's voice was fading as was she.

"Take your mother home, girls." Ella told the twins, Kara and Sarah. She watched as they left. There was something off about Barb, even counting the circumstances. She seemed nervous, edgy, clinging to her daughters and that was upsetting to Ella. She seemed to be afraid and she wasn't when Ella saw her yesterday or even this morning, so why was she now?

"Everyone's gone. We can leave now," Catherine said as she approached Ella. "What's wrong?"

"It's Barb. I feel she is afraid and I don't know why." Ella said frowning. Ella had a sixth sense with people and her feelings were almost always right.

"Maybe it's going back to the townhouse. She can come back and stay with me longer, if she needs to." Catherine said. "The twins are going back to university in the morning, so I will call her tonight."

"That's a good idea," agreed Maggie coming up to them. "I don't think I would want to stay where I found my dead husband, even a good dead husband and Ron certainly wasn't that."

They all agreed, nodding. Catherine was worried. She had spent quite a bit of time with

Barb over the past week and afraid was not a word to describe her friend's attitude. Upset yes, but not afraid. Even this morning she was just tired, hoping to get through the funeral and then get on with living her life. So, if she was now afraid, something must have happened.

Catherine had noticed the last man in the reception line, just because he was the last one before the service started. She had been watching over her friend and knew she was waning. What had he said to Barb when he leaned in toward her? Whatever it was seemed to take out any energy she had left. Catherine would talk to her. She had taken a picture of the man with her cell phone, so she would find out who he was. The other big question for Catherine was whether Barb knew of Ron's illegal activities. Catherine would bet she didn't, but she had been wrong before in her life. In her job, Catherine had learned not to be surprised at what people would do for money, fame or envy.

Catherine by Evonne D. Haley

Chapter 11

Barb sat with her daughters, Kara and Sarah, on either side of her on the couch in the condo drinking tea. She had paid for special cleaners to come in and clean her home, but she couldn't get his body lying there on the floor out of her mind.

"Do you want to sell the townhouse, Mom?" asked Sarah.

"Yes, I think I will, honey," she replied as she put her teacup down on the coffee table in front of her. She took both her daughter's hands in hers "But I will get us a three-bedroom condo, so you both will have a home with me as long as you want."

Both girls hugged her.

"Thank you, Mom," said Kara. "Life will be better for you now. We know how hard it was to live with him and we will both come home more often to spend time with you. We would have done that before, but it always seemed to make things worse for you."

"I would love that, girls, and I hope you come home often, but don't feel you have to come to babysit me. I know you are busy at school and I will be fine. I have Catherine and the girls to look out for me. They have been so great through all of this, especially Catherine. I don't think I could have handled it all without her support."

"Yeah, she has been great, plus we got to see all their kids and catch up with everyone," agreed Sarah.

"Have the police found out who killed him, Mom?" asked Kara quietly in her soft voice.

Kara was the one who was most affected by her father's anger and violence. She had become timid and withdrawn as a small child. Sarah was more aggressive and had pushed back. She didn't take his crap and he had never hit her. Maybe, because he was afraid of her. He had been a weasel of a man, about five feet seven inches tall and Sarah could have taken him. When she was fifteen, she decided to take self defense classes. She excelled at them and her attitude toward her father had changed then.

One day he was being particularly nasty with Kara.

"You are such a wimp, Kara. You're scared of your own shadow," and he pushed her.

Sarah came into the room and charged him, pushing him back.

"Come on, come get some from someone who isn't afraid of you, you bully," Sarah was not just furious. She was ready to kill him or least do him physical harm.

Ron looked at her and backed away. He saw the anger and the intent behind the anger. He knew. And he never touched either of them again.

Barb sighed. She felt so guilty for putting them through a life with him, but that would change now. They were great girls and had their whole lives ahead of them. She was so proud of them. But she still had to protect

67

them from Ron, what he had done and that man who was at the funeral.

"No, I haven't heard anything from the police yet," Barb answered Kara. "Don't worry, honey. I'm sure they will find whoever did it. They think it was probably a burglar your father surprised when he came home early." She reassured them. That was the story she had told them. They didn't need to know anything else about their father. They knew enough to give them nightmares as it was.

Barb drove the girls to Bishop Airport downtown the next morning. They had exams coming up at university just before Christmas, and she insisted they go back to study. She would be very busy selling the townhouse and her work would double until she hired a new consultant. She had an appointment with Maggie at eleven a.m. to list the property and this afternoon she was going to contact all Ron's clients to reassure them that their money was safe and she would be personally handling their accounts until she hired a new account manager.

Barb was so deep in thought she didn't notice she had missed her turn and was further downtown in a more undeveloped area. Suddenly a black Mercedes sedan pulled up beside her and cut her off. She slammed on her breaks and stopped. Her passenger door opened and the man from the funeral got in.

"I see you got the girls off on their flight this morning," he smiled at her. "Such pretty young girls."

"What do you want?" Barb was scared. This man was threatening without even trying to be.

"I want the money your husband stole. I'm sure you know what I am talking about."

"No, I don't know what you are talking about. We are financial consultants. We look after other people's money, but only on paper. We don't physically handle anyone's money." Barb was really scared. Oh, God. What had Ron done?

The man looked at her, studying her face. He could usually tell if someone was lying and he didn't think she was; but that made it worse. There was no sense in intimidating her because she didn't have the information he needed. She was really scared though and that told him she believed Ron had taken the money. He would use that fear to get her to find it. It would be in a Cayman account or a Swiss one probably. Somewhere Ron had the account numbers and access codes. He had to find the money before Sameer did something terrible like kidnapping her girls and using them to force her to give him the money. He would not be gentle with them; he would hurt them.

"Ron stole money from a man named Sameer and Sameer is not a nice man. He won't care what he has to do to get it back. Now, I am a more patient and forgiving man, and I know you will find the money and this will all go away. So, Barbara, you will go to your office and you will find where Ron hid the money. You will not tell anyone about this; no one. To ensure your silence a man named Geb will be watching your two lovely daughters at school. He is on the plane with them and he will protect them from Sameer for now. Do you understand?"

"Yes. What name would the accounts be under? I need more information." Barb's voice was shaking as much as she was.

"The main account will be under the Syrian Way, an NPO, a non-profit organization. I am sending my associate, Seth, to your office today at one o'clock. He will help you look. The files could be on a memory stick or on his computer, although I doubt he would put it where anyone could see it. The sooner you find what I need, the sooner this will all go away."

He paused to look at her, "You really are a beautiful woman." Then he left the car.

Barb sat in her car and watched him drive away. That man had just made a very big mistake. He had threatened her girls.

Getting her bearings, Barbara drove to her meeting with Maggie to list her townhouse.

"Barbara, how are you doing?" asked Maggie as Barb came into her office. "Honey, you are so pale. Sit down. Can I get you something? What's wrong?"

Maggie came around her desk to hug Barb. Barb's fearful gaze searched Maggie's.

"Please call Catherine to come. I am in trouble. Ron's death didn't free me from him and now my girls are in danger, as well. Only Catherine can help me." Barb started sobbing. She had just reached her limit and those little purple beets were wobbling through the aisles of her mind.

"Ok, hang on, honey." Reassured Maggie as she dialed Catherine. "We need you here a.s.a.p., Catherine. Barb's in trouble."

"She will be here in five minutes, Barb."

Catherine's office was on the seventeenth floor in the same office building as Maggie's.

"Here, have some water," Maggie passed her a bottle of water from her mini fridge. "I don't know why, but water always seems to help."

Catherine walked into Maggie's office and sat down beside Barb.

"What's going on, Barb?" she asked as she took her hand in hers.

"Ron stole someone's money and he wants it back."

"Is it the man from the funeral; the last one in line that upset you?"

"Yes, he said Ron stole money from a man named Sameer and he has someone called Geb watching my girls. He got on the plane with them this morning. What am I going to do, Catherine? I have to protect my girls!" Barb was starting to get angry.

"Sameer, he said Sameer. Are you sure, Barb, that's the name he gave?"

"Yes, Sameer, and he said he wasn't a nice man. Who is he?" asked Barb.

This wasn't good, thought Catherine. Sameer was a suspected terrorist and he wouldn't care what he had to do to get the money back. He had killed Ron. And that still puzzled Catherine. Why would he do that before he got his money back? Did someone get trigger happy? Did they think Barb knew where it was? Was that why they left him on Barb's living room floor? If so, Barb and her girls were in serious danger.

"Catherine, I know you're more than a lawyer, that you also work with the police some. Can you help me? Help my girls?"

"Honey, yes I will help you. I work some with the Justice Department. We know about Sameer. If Ron took his money, he must have had the account numbers and passwords to access them. We have his computer; well, cloned his computer before I turned it over to the police and we are still searching the files on it. We will find the money, Barb. I will also put some of my best people on watch to protect the girls immediately and discretely so Sameer won't know they are there.

Now, do you know the name of the man from this morning? Did he give you any information to help you find the accounts?"

"No, I don't know his name, but he said the account would be under the Syrian Way, a non-profit organization. Are you sure you can protect the girls?" Barb was regaining her composure and with it her anger with Ron. "I knew Ron wasn't scrupulous and I watched him closely with our clients, but I never dreamt he would do something like this. Is it just a matter of finding the right files?"

"No, it's a bit more complicated than that. We have the files on some of the money, but to get access to those bank accounts, you must have the account numbers and passwords. Ron most likely transferred money to overseas banks or to the Cayman Islands. He also didn't use names or bank transit numbers, just account numbers in his files, so we don't know where the accounts are or which banks they are in or even the country." Catherine was trying to explain how complicated this was to help her in her search at the office.

"So, what we need to find is really just the right banks and the account names to match the account numbers. He could have hidden that anywhere! How are we going to do this? I don't even know where to start. It wasn't in his computer?" asked Barb.

"No, we haven't found it yet, but we will. We think he must have had a code or legend hidden somewhere. He wasn't a stupid man, intellectually, but he was one to go up against Sameer. However, he left a clear paper trail of his dealings with Sameer. It looks like he may have even thought of blackmailing him at one point and then decided to go for the whole amount. Now that I know who he was dealing with, I have other places I can investigate. I just don't know why Sameer killed Ron before he got his money back." Catherine didn't dwell on this point or the fact that Ron was posed on her living room floor, as that was a clearly stated threat to Barb and Catherine didn't want to frighten her more than she was already.

"We need to search your house and the office, Barb. Can we go in this afternoon?"

Catherine by Evonne D. Haley

"Yes, you can, but that man said he is sending a man named Seth to the office at one this afternoon. I am supposed to say I hired him to take over some of Ron's accounts. Oh, Lord, what am I going to do? I can't breathe!" Barb was rocking in her chair with her hands over her face.

Catherine rubbed her back trying to calm her.

"Honey, you are going to act like nothing is happening. Just let him do his search at the office. Ron wouldn't have kept anything that important there, I am sure of that. Your computers are all networked so everyone has access? Right?"

"Right, but you have his laptop. That's where he would have kept the information. Even I couldn't get into his files there. He had everything password protected. Oh, what if this Seth wants the laptop? What do I tell him?"

"You tell him the police took it for the investigation," advised Catherine. "Stick to the truth. It's easier."

77

"Ok, I'd better go. I have to go hire Seth," Barb grimaced a smile as she got up to leave.

"It'll be alright, Barb. I 'm glad you came to me. Some of my men will be there to meet the girls` plane when it lands. Tonight, Maggie and Ella are coming over to cheer you up and help you move some of your stuff and Max in with me until your house sells. I have great security and you'll be safe there. OK?"

"Ok, thanks so much, Catherine. I don't know what I would do without you all." Barb hugged her and Maggie as she left.

"She can't take any more stress. I pray for God to give her strength." Maggie was worried about their friend.

"Me, too," stated Catherine, "and to keep her girls safe."

Catherine went back to work and knocked on her boss's office door, entering at his command.

"Got a minute, Boss?" she asked.

"Sure, what's up?"

"The Sameer case and Ron Delong's murder are connected," she said and proceeded to bring him up-to-date on the events.

"Well, I wasn't expecting that, but we did think there must be a money man to coordinate the funds." He sat back in his office chair touching his fingers together in front of his face. He was an attractive man and gave off an aura of power. He should. He was the Director of the CSIS, Canadian Security Intelligence Service that handled domestic security.

"Yes, well I told Barb Delong I would send someone to protect her daughters, discretely, so Sameer won't know we know yet. Do you want me to work jointly with the TOPD? They have Delong's laptop." She pointed out.

"Yes, work with them and keep me posted, up-to-date reports," he commander her. His caseload had just increased. Nothing new.

Chapter 12

Detective Jeremy Slade answered his office phone.

"There's a lady on her way up to see you," announced the desk sergeant from downstairs.

"Thanks, Sergeant," responded Slade as the elevator doors opened and Catherine stepped forward. She headed straight to his office. Man, she was beautiful! She exuded confidence in her stride and her eyes met his.

"Come in, Catherine. Have a seat. Coffee?" he offered as he sat back in his chair.

"No, thanks. How are you doing with Ron Delong's laptop? Anything interesting?" Catherine was testing the waters to see how much he would share.

"Not yet. We are having trouble breaking through the firewalls; which is weird, because our tech guys are good, really good. Why do you ask?" Slade knew she was either fishing or she had more information for him. He had the feeling it was the latter. She was the most unorthodox lawyer he knew.

"Ok, I may be able to help with that. My boss wants us to work together on this as our cases have collided." She slid her shield from CSIS across his desk to him. "And Barb Delong and her girls are now being threatened. Before you yell," she held her hand up to stop him from yelling, "I just found out an hour ago."

She proceeded to bring him up-to-date.

''We have intel on a terrorist named Sameer, who we believe is here in the city and is planning an attack. Although we have clues, which we will get into in a minute, we don't know where or when. We suspect he is here working with someone in the city, who is moving his money for him. Some of the money is coming from bogus websites begging for humanitarian aid for mid-east victims of ISIS. These sites are online for very short periods of time and then they disappear as do the bank accounts and the money that goes into them. The bank accounts must be set up legally, probably using many shell companies within shell companies; and, as long as the deposits are under $10,000, they are not flagged. We knew if we could get just one legitimate name we could use it as the string to find the money guy and that would bring us one step closer to Sameer." Catherine paused.

"And did you find him or the string?" prompted Slade frowning and then his expression changed. "Delong. You think Delong was the money man!"

"Yes, I know it was Delong for two reasons. One, Delong kept a detailed account of his dealings with Sameer on his laptop...."

"And just how could you possibly know that?" interrupted Slade. His voice was quiet and deep and yet Catherine knew he was seriously irate. Before she could answer, he did, "That's why you had it overnight before you, so generously, turned it in."

"Yes, sorry about that, but I was trying to protect Barb from whatever Ron had done to get himself murdered. He was not only an idiot but a dangerous idiot, and I figured he had done something illegal with some of their client's money. I still wouldn't have put this all together without Peter Petrov coming to the funeral and warning Barb about Sameer. I didn't recognize Petrov at the funeral, but when he was leaving, I took several pics of him on my phone and we identified him this morning. I will fax them over to you."

"Thank you. So kind of you. And what is the other reason?" Slade was not exactly angry. He felt betrayed and used.

"He told Barb the files would be under the Syrian Way. That is what sealed the identification. This was the only name we knew and that wasn't one hundred percent sure because the site was already closed down. We now have a name to use to try to connect the dots. Delong may have even used some of his legitimate clients' money for donations to the bogus non-profit organizations, claiming it was a tax write off. This clearly tells me he was going to run with all of Sameer's money, because by the end of February all of it would have come to light at tax time. There would have been no tax receipts for his real clients for those donations. The problem is that although Ron kept exact details of the money transfers from his legitimate clients, he kept everything else in code using numbers of accounts, dates and amounts, but no names, not even the banks he used."

Catherine was mad at Delong. It was bad enough that he ripped off the clients of Barb's company; he had put his whole family in jeopardy. He knew who he was dealing with; and he left Barb holding the bag, knowing they would go after her.

"Petrov stopped Barb this morning downtown and threatened her girls. He has someone watching them at their university and is putting a man called Seth in her office to try to find the money. The only good thing is that it is Petrov and not Sameer who is threatening her. Sameer would torture her or the girls to get what he wants. Petrov knows there are real repercussions for doing that in Canada so he will use threats and intimidation, at least at first. Now we know why Delong's body was left in their living room. Petrov knows that Sameer thinks Barb knows where the money is. We have to find the money and take down Sameer."

"And there is nothing you can use to arrest him? Do you have anyone on him?" Slade was frowning.

"Yes, now that we know Petrov is involved, we can watch him and see who he is working with, who his friends are and which terrorists he is dealing with. We also have a protection detail on the twins and Barbara." Catherine admitted. "If they are further threatened, we will intervene and put them in a safe house. I would rather use just surveillance so we can see how many more are in Sameer's cell and get ids on them, but I won't put Barb or her girls in any more danger."

"How is Barb doing with all of this?" asked Slade.

"She's doing ok, more upset about the girls being dragged into this and their safety than anything. Although the damage Ron may have done to the firm's name is unsettling, she will cope with it. Plus having the man, Seth, sent to her workplace must be nerve wracking."

"I got the impression she is a strong woman. She helped build and operates a successful financial firm, protected her kids from a violent husband for twenty years, and now is coping with all of this. You know I need to interview her again. You can sit in if you want as long as you don't interfere with the process." Slade threw her a bone. If they had to work together on this case, he had to get over her deceit with the briefcase.

"Ok, just please don't push her too hard. There are some questions I have as well. Why don't we do the interview at my house, make it informal, less intimidating for her?" Catherine was not quite begging.

"Alright, as long as I get some answers," agreed Slade. "Let's make it tomorrow morning at nine thirty."

Catherine by Evonne D. Haley

"Fine. I will set it up," said Catherine as she stood up to leave.

Slade came around his desk and helped her put her coat on. She was so close he could smell her hair. It smelled like flowers. He was very attracted to this woman. She was smart, confident, beautiful and warm. Although she could be devious, she really cared about her friend. He would like to get to know her better.

Catherine could smell his aftershave as he helped her on with her coat. It was a masculine scent that gave her shivers down to her toes. His hands closed onto her shoulders a moment before he let go of her. He was a gentle man, yet strong and powerful. His occupation could have left him disillusioned with people, but he seemed to have balanced the good and evil parts of humanity with an attitude of caring. He liked his job; he liked helping people, giving back by taking the criminals off the street, seeing justification for the innocent. Catherine liked him more each

time she interacted with him. She looked
forward to seeing him again.

Chapter 13

Maggie and Ella helped Barb pack to move in with Catherine. The townhouse was very, very tidy, very little clutter, almost minimalistic. The only rooms that looked lived in were the ones Barb used as an office and her bedroom. There were pictures of the twins from babies to college with a few collectibles, including shells from the beach and the weird looking ceramic pig they had given her years ago.

"I am only packing this room and my bedroom. The artwork on the walls goes to the auction house. They are coming tomorrow afternoon to pack it all up," explained Barb.

"What about this little box? It looks old, like a Chinese puzzle box, could be valuable." Ella said as she twisted the box in her hand. "Reminds me of a Rubik's Cube."

"Yes, it's going with the art work to be sold at auction. It's Ron's and I am not taking anything of his. Oh, that's not true. I am taking his wine collection. You guys can help me drink it." She looked over at the box in Ella's hands. "It is supposed to have a secret compartment in it, but I've never been able to find it. You take it, Ella. You're good at solving puzzles. Maybe you can figure it out."

"Are you sure? It might be valuable." Protested Ella.

"I am sure. It is a thank you gift." Barb stated firmly.

When the girls finished packing Barb's things, they all headed to Catherine's. Maggie and Ella were traveling together in her car.

"Maggie, did you notice Barb's life in that house? She only lived in two rooms, her office and her bedroom. I didn't know things were so bad between her and Ron that they practically lived apart. Did you?" Ella was concerned. Every room in Ella's house was clearly lived in and it showed in the organized chaos of her home.

"No, I didn't either. I guess once the girls went to university, they didn't bother with pretence any longer."

Catherine by Evonne D. Haley

Ella looked out the car window as they drove down Young Street. She watched the lights of the skyscrapers fall behind block after block. Storefronts advertised Christmas in all its commercialism. As she got older Ella found it sad that the real meaning of Christmas was smothered in buying gifts instead of celebrating the birth of Christ. Even Christmas cards were now mostly reading Happy Holidays so that soon 'Christ' would disappear from Christmas altogether. And what a terrible thing it was to see God's love being pushed aside as people tried to keep pace with their busy lives, like rats on a treadmill, not seeing anything but the narrow path in front of them, the never ending repetition of work and responsibilities and not the love that was available to them. They didn't even have to do anything to get it; all they had to do was accept it as the truth.

Chapter 14

At nine-thirty the next morning, Slade arrived for his interview with Barbara Delong at Catherine's home. It was in an informal setting where Barb would be more comfortable with Catherine there in attendance to support her.

"Come in, Detective Slade," invited Catherine. "Let me have your coat.   You can go in and take a seat. Barb's waiting in the living room."

She put her hand on his arm as he started to go by her. "Please, be gentle with her. She has been through a lot."

Slade met her eyes. He nodded recognizing the worry there for her friend. Barbara stood as he entered the living room.

"Hello, Detective Slade," she greeted him softly.

"Hello, Mrs. Delong. Please sit and relax. This won't be an interrogation. I just want to clear up a few questions I have." He smiled at her to put her at ease.

"Please call me Barb," she said.

"My first name is Jeremy, but most people call me Slade." He wanted her to be comfortable with him.

Catherine came in and smiled as she sat down on the couch by Barb.

Slade looked at Barb and said, "Did Ron normally take Max for walks?"

Barb felt fuzzy for a minute. She thought his questions would be more concentrated on Ron's business practices.

"No, he hated her. He would be more inclined to kick her out of his way, which is why I was so surprised to see her on the doorstep that night. I don't know why he would have taken her out."

"Ok, did you know all of his clients? Did you work together on all the accounts? Had you met them all personally either in the office or at social functions?"

"I know all of our established clients who had previously been my father's, but not all of the new clients Ron had brought in. My father established the firm forty years ago. I just took over ten years ago when he retired after his second heart attack."

Well, thought Slade, the 'I' in that last sentence was telling, even though the firm was called Carter and Delong, she classed it as hers.

"What was your firm called when your father was president and CEO?"

"It was Carter Consultants, Inc. when my father started it. About fifteen years ago Dad put me on the letterhead as Carter & Delong, Inc. After Dad died Ron wanted to go to Delong & Delong, Inc." explained Barb, "but since Dad had established the firm, I wanted his name kept and I felt the clients wouldn't like the change either."

"Where did Ron work previously to joining your firm?"

Catherine by Evonne D. Haley

"He worked in New York at a firm called FCI, Financial Consultants, Inc. as a financial advisor. I met him at a conference there, we started dating long distance and then he was transferred to Toronto. After we married, he stayed at their Toronto firm for about two years and then worked for a couple of other financial firms until he came on board with us."

"Did your father like him?" Slade was starting to get a more detailed description of Ron Delong's character.

"Not at first, but I think he was more comfortable about him before he died five years ago." Barb was not looking at him when she made that statement.

I doubt Ron would have ever measured up to Dad even after fifty years, thought Slade. Ron was transferred from New York, the capital of the financial world, to Toronto, which meant he was demoted; and Slade doubted Ron asked for the transfer because of his love for Barb. The picture he was getting of Ron was that he was a user of people, a scam artist just one step ahead of the law in his professional life and a bully in his personal life, especially, regarding his wife and daughters and even Max. Slade would get a more detailed background on Delong, but his sense of people was rarely wrong. And Barb's comment was telling. She had said her Dad was more comfortable *about* Ron before he died. Not with, but about, which told Slade Barb's father had serious reservations with Ron's character and his joining the firm; plus, they didn't change the name of the firm after Barb's father died. Although, when a company had been established for over forty years, you usually would not change the name as you would have so much reputation built up in it.

Slade decided to push Barb on this issue.

"Did Ron want to change the name? Was he angry about it?" asked Slade.

"Yes, he felt his name should be on the letterhead," she answered simply.

"But you are President of the company?" Slade wanted clarification on Barb's position in the company.

"Yes, and CEO. Dad wanted it that way," she confirmed.

Smart Dad, thought Slade. However, he sensed Barb would never have put Ron's name on the letterhead and that must have rankled him.

"How was your marriage going; any problems?" Slade was getting more personal.

"What do you mean?" Barb seemed uncomfortable with this question.

"Did you get along? Have fights? Was he ever violent with you?" Slade's questions were getting closer to home.

"Is this line of questioning pertinent to the case?" interrupted Catherine.

"Yes, I am trying to get a sense of Ron's character to see who would have motive to kill him." Slade raised his eyebrows at Catherine. He knew she knew what he was doing. Then he realized she was giving Barb a minute to form her replies.

"Barb?"

She looked at him with determination in her eyes as she lifted her chin and spoke. "Ron was not a great husband or father," she said softly.

"Continue," encouraged Slade.

"Things were good at first. Then he started hitting me whenever he got angry, but after the twins were born, I told him I would go home to Dad if he ever did it again. The physical abuse stopped, but he was a bully to me and the girls. When they were just teenagers, Sarah stood up to him and he left them alone after that. The girls had taken self defense classes. Sarah excelled at them and I think he knew Sarah could seriously harm him. After that he spent less time at home and it was better for a while."

"You never wanted to leave him? It sounds like you would have had your father's support then and you would have had the money now."

Slade was always amazed at the reasons women had for staying with abusive husbands; and he didn't just mean physical abuse, but mental and emotional abuse, too.

"It was complicated. We worked together at the firm. It would have damaged it. We are a small company with a few very, very wealthy clients. Most of the clients Dad had acquired were old money, very conservative. Some didn't think a woman should be running the company, but Dad had reassured them that he had complete faith in me. After Dad died I worked very hard to keep those clients. Divorcing Ron would have resulted in losing some of them. They were the solid base of the company in more ways than just money. They gave the company recognition and respect. Dad didn't work for more accounts as he was satisfied with the revenue we brought in. But after Dad died, Ron started actively working on acquiring new clients.

I was working on buying Ron out, but he didn't want that. The company gave Ron the status he wouldn't have otherwise had. Then the girls went off to university and it was easier. We were more like roommates. At work, we were cordial. Ron could be charming and our employees liked him. He knew how to make clients trust him." Barb paused.

"Yes? Had his demeanor or actions changed lately, Barb?"

"Sort of. In the last year or so he had become more secretive. He went out for a lot of meetings that he said were meetings with prospective clients, but they never seemed to solidify into accounts and he was vague about who they were. There were two new clients that I have never met. Ron had put them in the system at work with just their contact information. One was the director of the Syrian Way."

"I will need that information, Barb," Slade interrupted and she nodded.

"But the biggest change was when Ron started working on his laptop, even at work and always took it wherever he went. All the computers at work are networked for easier access to files. Ron stopped using his desktop computer and said he would put the new clients into the system when the accounts were firmed up."

"I will need access to all your files, Barb. I will use discretion to maintain your clients' privileged information." When she didn't respond, he said, "I can get a subpoena if necessary."

"That would be best, I think," agreed Barb, "to be acceptable to my clients. This is going to hurt my firm, isn't it?"

"I can get the authorization, Detective Slade, through the Justice Department," offered Catherine.

"OK, that is acceptable," agreed Slade. "Had Ron's spending habits changed? Had he become more extravagant in his purchases, new cars, wardrobe?"

"Not that I noticed. I don't think so unless he was hiding them from me." She paused, "He traveled more lately, a lot really when I think about it."

101

"Do you know where he went?"

"No, but I can get the information, if he booked through the firm," Barb offered.

"Did Ron have a girlfriend?" asked Slade abruptly.

"Not that I know of," Barb said as she met his gaze steadily.

"Is there anyone in your life, Barb?"

"You mean a boyfriend? No, there isn't." She affirmed with a smile, "One man was enough for me."

"Don't write us all off for one bad relationship, Barb. You are a lovely woman with many years ahead of you to share with someone." Slade stood. "I think that's all for now. I will get back to you, if I have any more questions."

"I'll walk out with you," said Catherine rising.

"Oh, here comes Max." She bent to pick up the tiny pup. "How are you, sweetie? You're walking without limping, that's good."

Slade put out his hand for the Yorkie to sniff. She whined and wiggled until he took her from Catherine. Then she snuggled up to his neck and sighed.

Both Catherine and Barb just stood and gaped at him.

"She has never gone to a man before," said Barb. "She really likes you."

"Dogs like me. All kinds. I was raised on a farm and had a good rapport with all the animals. My Dad used to say I was the animal whisperer. Plus, Max is an easy pup to love. She is very affectionate, aren't you Max?" he said as he stroked her.

Max just burrowed into his chest more, like she was trying to get inside him and sighed again. Slade sat back down, looked at Barb and Catherine and said, "I will be honest with you both. I am sure Ron hid Sameer's money. We have his laptop and we think we know how he did it, but we don't know where he put it. I also think from what you tell me that he was planning to run with it.

103

It looks like Ron got involved with Petrov on some shady money deal a couple years ago. Then Petrov hired him to set up the website, the Syrian Way, to funnel money through it for Sameer. Money came in to the website account and Ron transferred it out to unknown accounts.

The money was supposed to be transferred through shell companies to overseas accounts for Sameer to buy guns, ammo and materials for bombs from Petrov and travel contingencies for terrorists to come into Toronto for an attack. The money disappeared and only Ron knew where. Petrov didn't get paid for the supplies and Sameer cannot get access to them as Petrov won't give them to him without the money.

Petrov's man is not going to find it at the office so just let him search; then he will leave. However, we cannot arrest them without linking them to the funds and Ron has hid that by just using numbered accounts. We need to find the key to positively link Sameer to the illegal money transactions. If Petrov hadn't come after you, Barb, at the funeral, we couldn't have linked him to Sameer. Now we can. Your girls are protected at university as are you with Catherine. Stay with her until this is over and it will be. Hopefully, soon."

Chapter 15

Peter Petrov stood looking out at downtown Toronto, a city with over four million souls, block after block of skyscrapers that reached to the sky and red taillights of traffic clogged at five o'clock rush hour. His mind kept going to Barbara Delong and the money. He wished he had gotten to Delong before Sameer killed him. He would have made him suffer longer for all the aggravation he had caused him and now Barb. When he was under duress, Ron told Sameer Barb had the money, and he believed him. By killing him and putting his body in the condo, Sameer was sure would frighten Barb into giving him the money, but she didn't. Not even after her daughters were threatened. Now Petrov had his doubts she even knew about the money. If Ron had lied, he really must have hated his wife. He put a target on her back knowing what Sameer would do to get his money back.

"I don't have your money; Barb has it," swore Ron and then he laughed. But it was the look in his eyes that startled Petrov. You would expect to see fear or even regret on a dying man's face, but what Petrov had seen was glee, satisfaction. It had unnerved him. Then before he could stop him, Sameer had shot Delong. As a result, Petrov would have to kill Sameer, but not until they had found the money.

Chapter 16

Barb sat staring at her office door with Max on her lap. She was bringing her to work with her instead of leaving her at Catherine's house alone all day. Max was acting nervous and clingy and cried if she left her alone. Barb had her small doggy bed under her desk and when she had clients, she just put Max there. It was working well. Max was also a calming influence on Barb.

As she sat there now at her desk stroking Max, she was able to think calmly. What should she do now? She had searched the townhouse from top to bottom and found nothing besides dust; and she had searched thoroughly, as she packed up her home for sale. The problem was she wasn't even sure of what she was looking for.

She had lied to Detective Slade. Her and Ron's relationship had started out so well. They were in love, or so she had thought. The work week seemed to drag on relentlessly until the weekend when they were together either in

Toronto or New York. When Ron had told her, he had gotten the transfer to Toronto to be near her, she was ecstatic. Their wedding was a dream. Her father was wary of Ron at first, but seemed to come around. Then Ron started slapping her whenever he got mad; but when the twins were born, everything changed. Ron changed. To say he was not paternal was an understatement. He didn't want anything to do with them. They took up all of Barb's time and attention and when she was not caring for them, she was too tired to do anything with him. Eventually, he took his wants elsewhere, but it wasn't satisfying. He wanted Barb. She was his wife. Consequently, he just took what he wanted, when he wanted it. At first, if she objected, he slapped her. If she objected strongly, he would beat her. She stopped objecting. Eventually, he started hitting her just because he felt like it. He was smart; he hit her where no one could see the bruises. She began wearing high-necked blouses with long sleeves so the ones on her arms didn't show as well as the bruises on her neck where he choked her.

In the beginning, Barb was stunned at his behaviour; she blamed herself. She had ignored him somewhat when the twins were born. He didn't give her any help and it was time consuming caring for two babies, as well as exhausting. When her father offered to hire some help for her, Barb wanted to accept his generosity, but she didn't want anyone to see or tell him how Ron treated her. So, she told him she was doing fine, even though she was barely functioning.

During the day, while Ron was at work and the twins slept, she tried to rest, but the house was a mess and Ron complained if she didn't keep it spotless. Sometimes, she would fall asleep if she sat down for just a minute on the sofa. When the twins were about five months old, they finally started sleeping through the night. Before that they needed to be fed every two to three hours to bring up their low birth weight.

Barb had taken a year of maternity leave, but when the babies were eight months old, she started working from home some. Then her father had a heart attack and she went back full time. She hired a nanny/housekeeper. Although she had some qualms leaving the twins, she needed to be at the office more.

By this time, she knew Ron would ruin her father's company if left to his own devices. It wasn't that he didn't know what he was doing, he did; but he took chances with other people's money, risky investments and even some illegal transactions. He was a genius at moving money and avoiding taxes, but their company wasn't built on that. A large part of their business was old, established clients with trust funds and safe investments. These people didn't take unnecessary risks with their money. It had been passed down generation after generation with every investment weighed for the continuity of future generations.

Barbara's father had been right. Left to run rampant through the company, Ron would have destroyed it. Barbara had maintained control of the company primarily because her father insisted on it; but she knew Ron, and her father was right. She should have listened to him. Now she had to go through all his client transactions and see what damage he had caused the firm and find those accounts Ron had stolen from.

She should have divorced Ron years ago, when her father was still alive. She would have had his support and it wouldn't have damaged the firm as much as it was going to now. She had loved Ron in the beginning. That was her first mistake.

Chapter 17

Maggie was in her office going through new listings on the market when she saw one for a condo in Catherine's building. That would be great for Barb, she thought. Good security, plenty of room for the girls and acceptable for Max. She would set up an appointment to show it to her. An hour later she called Barb at work and explained the situation.

"It's a beautiful condo, great views of the lake and downtown. Would you like to see it, Barb?"

"Yes, it sounds wonderful. When could I move in?" she asked.

As much as she loved Catherine and was grateful for her hospitality, she really wanted her own space and privacy.

"It is empty now, so immediately after the deal closes, which depends on you and your lawyer and how fast you can get the paperwork done." Stated Maggie.

"Let`s go see it. Can you take me now?" Barb had excitement in her voice for the first time in weeks, months really.

"Yes, I will meet you there in an hour." Maggie`s office was also downtown.  "It`s on the thirtieth floor, 3003. I can meet you in the lobby."

"Great, see you there."

An hour later after meeting Maggie, they toured the condo. Barb fell in love with the open floor plan, modern kitchen and the great room that was conducive to entertaining and being together with family; something that wasn't done in their old home, but something Barb planned and looked forward to doing with her girls and her friends. Maggie wrote up the sales contract and immediately faxed it to the seller's agent.

"When will I hear back?" Barb asked Maggie.

"I will call you as soon as I hear from them. It should be today or tomorrow. It's a great offer, Barb; full price and fast closing. It should be a done deal." Maggie was confident as she knew the seller's agent and had worked with him on many deals. Barb should be in her new home within a week to ten days depending on how fast her lawyer could get the paperwork ready. We will have to throw her a housewarming party, she thought. Maybe she would fly the twins home for the weekend when they held the party. It would be a great surprise for Barb and the girls could settle into the new home their mother promised she would always have for them.

Chapter 18

Slade was at his desk in the Toronto Police Department going through reports on the background check he had done on Ron Delong, his bank records, a DUI from sixteen years before, one disturbance of the peace report from his residence on Birch Street, also sixteen years before. This must have been the incident Barb had mentioned. She had refused to press charges, but her threat to go to her father must have worked or she just hid the abuse from everyone as there were no other reports. Maybe he realized he could lose the money train he was on and wised up, but Slade doubted it. Delong was a real sleaze ball, a bully and one step from being caught for illegal activities, including insider trading. It didn't take much convincing for Slade to believe he had stolen Sameer's money and was planning on absconding with it to a country with no extradition treaty. His banking records showed a man who earned very good money and spent every penny of it on cars, liquor, clothes, traveling and gambling. He went to Los Vegas several times a year and lost a lot of money there. He certainly lived beyond his means and his credit cards were all maxed out.

The bank showed he had another safety deposit key in just his name, not Barb's, which was not among his personal affects catalogued at the townhouse. There was, however, a key found on him that was not for his house or office, but was definitely a house key. Slade flipped to a report on his personal holdings and found nothing, not even his townhouse was in his name; it was in Barb's. There were no deeds in his name, but there was a lease that had his signature for an apartment downtown on Richmond Street East.

Now that is interesting, thought Slade. The reason a man kept an apartment aside from his residence was usually for a mistress or a place to take lovers. I wonder if his wife knew? She had said, "Not as far as I know" when Slade had asked if her husband had a girlfriend and he had believed her. Now he wondered if she had been honest with him.

If Ron had a girlfriend, did she know where Ron put the money? Was he planning on running with her or leaving her behind as well as his wife and family? Slade needed to find out who she was and interview her. The first place he would look was at the apartment. If she wasn't there, he would put a watch on it, to see who came and went.

Chapter 19

Catherine had just filed a request through the Justice Department for a subpoena to go through Barb's company files. As she was heading to her boss's office to bring him up-to-date on the case, she saw Slade getting off the elevator. When he saw her, he veered toward her.

"Come into my office, Slade," she said as she changed direction and went back to her office as he followed her.

"I thought we could catch up on the case," he said as he sat down in front of her desk.

"Ok, you go first," she smiled at him with eyes that sparkled.

She really was beautiful, so alive, he thought and smiled back at her.

"We found out that Delong had a second safety deposit box, but haven`t found the key to it yet. Maybe Barb has it?"

"I can ask her if she knows where it is," Catherine offered. She made a note.

119

"We also found a key on him that goes to an apartment on Richmond Street East."

"Really? That's a surprise. I wonder if Barb knows about it?"

"My thoughts exactly. Do you want to ask her or do you want me to interview her again?" Slade asked.

"No, I will ask her tonight. She has bought an apartment in my building and is moving in a week from Saturday. It is a new start for her, a place of her own where her girls can come home from school. She is really excited about it."

"Also, see if she knows about a girlfriend. I have a detail watching the apartment to see who comes and goes. I had asked her and she said she didn't know of one. She was a little evasive, so talk to her about it. She might open up with you more." Slade said as he smiled at her.

He really was a handsome man Catherine thought; a lot of boyish charm in the man.

"Would you have dinner with me tomorrow evening? We can compare notes again." Slade lifted his right eyebrow as he tried to persuade her.

"Is that the only reason you want to have dinner with me?" Catherine copied his raised eyebrow.

"No, I want to get to know you and I am grasping at straws to talk you into it," he grinned boyishly as he waited for her answer.

"Yes, I would like that, too." Catherine's response surprised her. She had been thinking of him a lot and was attracted to him, but she didn't think she was open to a relationship at this time in her life. Then again, maybe she was only open to him.

"Great. I will pick you up at seven. I know a great little place in China Town that serves authentic Chinese food. The owner is a friend so I'm sure we can get a table."

Slade didn't tell her how he had come to know the owner; that he had saved his son from joining a gang and helped him get into the police academy. Slade always had a table at the restaurant, no reservation needed.

"That sounds wonderful."

Slade got up to leave before she changed her mind. "See you tomorrow night then," he said as he left.

Catherine watched him leave with a new emotion going through her. She really did find him attractive, even the way he moved; his walk was strong, self-assured and confident like him. She was looking forward to seeing him in a more personal environment.

Just then her phone rang taking her from dreaming to reality.

"Catherine speaking," she answered.

"Hi. How's your day going?" greeted Maggie.

"Great, and yours?"

"Good. Busy. You know Barb bought the condo in your building and is moving in next weekend, so I thought we could bring the girls home to celebrate their new home."

"What a great idea, Maggie! I guess it will be a surprise for Barb?"

"Yes. I am calling the girls tonight to make the arrangements for their flight. We can plan the menu etc. next week when we have lunch with Ella. OK?"

"Sounds great, but let me make the travel arrangements with my agents who are watching them. Barb will love this. She has been going through such a hard time, it will be nice to have a party to celebrate with all our kids together. We will talk again soon, Maggie."

Catherine hung up thinking she had such great friends, kind, warm and giving, not like the people in the cases she worked to bring to justice. Some of them were pure evil, like Sameer.

••

Barb's intercom rang.

123

"You have a caller on line two, but he wouldn't give his name, just said you would want to speak to him."

"Ok, thanks, J.J. I'll take the call," Barb knew it was Petrov.

"Hello. Who is this?" she asked.

"Mrs. Delong. You were smart to take my call. How are your girls? My man, Geb, tells me they are good students, studying hard for their exams next week. You must be very proud of them. Beautiful girls as well, just like their mother. Have you found the money yet?" Petrov's voice was well modulated, almost charming, with no threat in his tone, but it was clearly meant.

"You will leave my girls alone, Mr. Petrov. Yes, I know who you are. I don't know anything about the money or where it is. The man you sent here couldn't find it either so just leave us alone!" Barb slammed the phone down and put her head in her hands. She probably shouldn't have hung up on him, but she was just so frustrated. Even though Ron was dead, he was still hurting her and the girls. Well, she wouldn't let Petrov hurt them. Barb did what she should have done sooner.

"Catherine? I need your help," she said to her on the phone. "Petrov is threatening the girls and I want them somewhere he can't reach them. I am afraid he will kidnap them to force me to tell him where Ron hid the money; and since I won't tell him, I am afraid he will hurt them. Sameer would, for sure, so I need them to be safe, to protect them from him." Barb's voice was shaking from rage, as well as fear.

"Alright, Barb. I have been thinking on this as well. I will take the girls into protective custody until this is resolved." Catherine assured her friend.

"When?" pushed Barb.

"Today," answered Catherine with a grim tone to her voice. "I will let you know as soon as they are safe, Barb." She didn't tell her that Sameer was on a deadline and the closer it came, the more dangerous he would become.

125

It was time to take the girls out of his reach. She would put this in action immediately.

"Thanks, Catherine. I don't know what I would do without you. I know I keep saying that and I am sorry to keep dumping all of this on you, but you are my only hope." Her voice broke on a sob. She was trying to keep it together and not break down completely. If Ron wasn't already dead, she might be incensed enough to kill him herself.

"You can lean on Detective Slade, as well, Barb. He is a good man and good at his job. If I am ever not available, don't hesitate to call him. Ok?"

"Alright. Thanks. I will wait to hear from you when the girls are safe."

Catherine sat at her desk after she hung up thinking of something Barb had said. Was it just semantics or was the wording a slip of the tongue? Was there a different meaning in her words or was Catherine tired and hearing truths that weren't there. Barb had said, "Sameer would for sure." How did Barb know that or was she just saying something she had heard Catherine say?

She was tired. The more she looked into Petrov, the more she learned how dangerous he was. He appeared to be a thriving business man; and until you broke down his life, including his friends and his business associates, you couldn't see the complete picture of Peter Petrov. He had safeguards on his communications, but Catherine's people were some of the best in the world. Practically nothing could stop them given time and with the technology they had access to and their skills, nothing was safe from their prying eyes.

Catherine had hired one of the best hackers in the world out of prison. Well, actually, she had kept him from going to prison. He had been caught hacking into the RCMP servers and was going away for quite a while. Catherine saw the potential in him to work for the government doing what he did best and she pulled enough strings to commute his sentence to work for her organization. His name was Craig and he was only seventeen years old. Without her intercession, he would have gone to prison for a long time and the repercussions of that would have ruined whatever life he would have had when he got out. He loved her for that and would have done anything for her.

Craig was now working solely on the Petrov/Delong case. He could find information online that no one else could, because no firewall could keep him out. He could hack through any server, business, military or government, including their satellites.

When he knocked on her door, she immediately knew he had found a threat of imminent danger to Barb's family.

"Petrov just sent orders to kidnap Delong's daughters. It looks like he is sending them to Russia. He has filed a flight plan on a private plane out of New York, tonight at ten p.m."

Catherine picked up her phone. "Thank you, Craig," she said as he left her office.

Her order on the phone was to activate her team at the girl's university to immediately take them to a safe house. The order was too late. The girls were missing and two of the men on the surveillance team were dead. She had sent a team of four men to watch the girls, two on, two off for twenty-four hours around the clock surveillance. The two men on duty were found dead in the trunk of their car by the other two agents when they came to relieve them.

"Do you know when this occurred?" she asked Frank, her lead man on the team.

"They were killed within the last two hours. I am so sorry, Catherine. We had no warning he would make this move. The surveillance team I have on Petrov still has eyes on him so he didn't do this himself, but he could have had someone else do it."

"Or it could be Sameer who has them. Ok, Frank. I'll take it from here and get back to you with new instructions as soon as I can." Catherine felt blindsided. She should have taken the threat to Barb's girls more seriously; she should have sent more men or taken them into custody sooner. What was she going to tell Barb? But first, she would call Slade with this new development. It was hard to stay calm. She loved those girls like they were her own. She closed her eyes and paused for a moment to pray for the girls. Please, Father, don't let any harm come to them. When she looked up Slade was standing by her.

"What's happened, Catherine?" he laid his hand gently on her back.

"I think Sameer has the girls. Why did you come back?" she asked.

"We had a tip that Sameer was going to make a move on the DeLongs. We thought it was on Barbara. I'm sorry about her girls." He said softly, "We need to pool our resources and form a task force. We are both investigating the same crime really. Mine is focused on Delong's murder and yours is on Sameer's activities, which is now centered on the reason for Delong's murder."

"Yes, I agree. We can use the large boardroom for gathering information and correlating it. We probably have better technology than you do. How many people from your office do you want to bring in? I have Craig, our in-house computer genius, Marianne, who is phenomenal sorting and compiling data, Fran, our financial expert, and as many support staff as we need." Finally, Catherine felt she was doing something constructive.

Slade nodded his agreement. He had no problem with her taking the lead. She was right; she did have better resources, but he had great people too.

"I'll bring four to begin with," he responded. "I have Roger, who is a genius putting people together, my chief of staff so to speak." He grinned self-consciously. "He can get them working together more efficiently. I have a financial analyst as well. Helen knows how money can be moved and has some new information on the Sharing Way that I was going to discuss with you tomorrow. Our dinner will only be delayed until the girls are home, by the way." He didn't say it as a question. Without waiting for an answer, he continued. "Sam is our resident computer expert; Ren is the smartest person I know. She has an encyclopedia as a brain. She remembers everything she sees and hears, plus she can read situations and forecast their outcomes to an astonishing degree. I can also bring four support staff to match yours."

"Ok, that is seventeen people to start with not including agents in the field; and we can add more, if needed. My first priority is to get the girls back unharmed and then to find the money. Sameer can't do anything without it and he's getting desperate. He is a sociopath with no empathy and he is not the kind of person you want to tick off. Killing to him is like brushing your teeth; just something to be done. I am praying we find the girls before he kills them. I'll set up the conference room and you can bring your people over right away."

Slade nodded. He knew she was feeling guilty over the girls' disappearance, but she was a professional, handling it in a positive, no nonsense manner to correct it. Still, he could tell she was worried. He put his hand on her shoulder.

"We will get them back, Catherine."

She nodded, but he saw the desperation in her eyes. Sameer was a dangerous man and he could have already killed the girls` father. He had nothing to lose by killing them too. Petrov's role in this was not yet understood. In many ways, it seemed he was trying to protect them, but did he need to protect them from himself as well as Sameer?

Chapter 20

Ella sat at her desk lost in thought, twisting the cube in her hands. Catherine had just called and told her about the girls. They would have to put the housewarming party on hold until they rescued them. What Barb was going through! How much stress could she take? Please, Father, be with her and bring the girls back safely, she prayed.

Just then the cube came apart in her hands. She had been pushing on the dots and turning it when it suddenly just came apart. Inside was a safety deposit key. She picked up the phone and called Catherine. Maybe this would help her with the case. Anything to help close it, so Barb and her family would be safe again.

While the rest of the task force was setting up in the conference room, Slade and Catherine were racing to the airport to take the CSIS jet to New York to rescue the Delong girls before Petrov could get them out of the

134

country. They had found out that Petrov had taken his jet to New York with a flight plan to continue on to Russia. It would take exact timing, because they had to wait for them to arrive at the airport, but not give them time to get on the plane.

This would be the most dangerous part of the plan for the girls. They would be in the cross fire between Petrov`s men and theirs. Getting close enough to grab them and get them out of the way was Slade's primary goal. Catherine's job was to provide support for Slade's men. Only after the girls were safe would they go after Petrov and his men. Another question that needed to be answered was 'where was Sameer'? Would he be leaving on the plane as well and how many people would he have with him?

"I know this will be dicey, Catherine, but we can do it. They don't know we know their plans, so we will have surprise on our side and it will only take those few seconds for us to succeed in getting the girls to safety."

"There are just so many things that can go wrong, Slade. I love those girls like they are my own. And that is the reason you are taking lead on this. You will have a cooler head when this all goes down and it never goes down like you plan."

"Our men are good. Professionals. They drill for this scenario. They will adapt to the situation and their job is to get the girls out of Petrov's hands. Then your men will go after Petrov and Sameer and only then. The girls' safety comes first." Slade was reassuring Catherine of their priorities.

"Alright. Let's go over the plan again. I want to be there waiting when they get to the airport and for this to run like clockwork."

Please God, keep them safe and help us bring them home safely, prayed Catherine.

The private airport was tiny, only two hangers, a small building that was used as an office and one runway. Currently there was only one private jet sitting at the end of the runway not far from the office building and it had the stairs down, ready for boarding.

Catherine's team was in place in the woods behind the office and she had a sniper on the roof. They had a clear view of the plane and its surroundings, but still no sign of Petrov. Slade's men were ready to go as soon as Petrov showed up with the girls. They had already cleared the hangers, subdued the man in the office and the pilot of the small jet before either could call out for help and replaced them with their own people.

"They are about a mile out, Slade," reported one of his team who was being the lookout dressed as a lineman in a cherry picker on the road leading into the airport.

"Ok, everyone knows the drill," commanded Slade. "We get the girls to safety first. Then we take Petrov and his men down as well as Sameer if he is here. We want them alive, if possible, so don't fire until fired upon. Petrov and Sameer both have information that we need to determine if there is still a threat to Toronto."

Three black SUVs roared up to the jet. Petrov's men got out of the first and last vehicles with guns raised and looked around. Then they opened the doors to the second vehicle and Petrov got out of the front and helped the girls from the back. They looked frightened and held onto each other. Petrov motioned for them to go up the steps into the plane and turned to his second in command to say something. Behind him the girls were pulled quickly into the plane and the stairs were immediately retracted.

Two of Petrov's men opened fire and were killed in the opening volley. One of Slade's was wounded, as Petrov and one of his men, Geb, ran to the hanger next to the plane and disappeared inside. Over the gunfire, Slade heard another sound, but he was pinned down and couldn't go after him.

Catherine's sniper had a night vision scope and now had targets that he quickly eliminated; two more down. The rest tried to escape in the SUVs, but Slade's men kept them pinned down. Under cover of the gunfire and men screaming as they were impacted with bullets, the roof of the hanger had opened and a helicopter rose quickly, cleared the hanger and escaped to the north; its quiet rotors showed it to be a new stealth bird. Petrov had more money or access to more money than they had thought, mused Slade as he watched it disappear. They had seen the helicopter, but didn't realize the roof retracted. That was an error on Slade's part.

He looked around. There were seven dead bodies, but none were his. One of his men was wounded, but not fatally.   He would recover. Petrov's men wouldn't.

Catherine walked over to him.

"It went better than I had hoped, but we didn't get Petrov. However, we got the girls and none of our men were killed. That's all that matters right now." She smiled at Slade.

Catherine by Evonne D. Haley

The all clear was heard from every direction and the stairs to the jet came back down. Catherine's man looked out and when she nodded, the twins were helped down from the plane. They both appeared confused and when they saw Catherine, they ran to her. She held them both to her tightly and told them everything was good now.

"You are safe now girls. It's OK. He won't get his hands on you again. We will keep you safe until this is all over and he is behind bars."

The girls were crying and nodding to her reassurances.

"We just want to go home to Mom," said Sarah.

"Yes, we are taking you there. She is at my place and it has great security so you will all be safe there."

Catherine looked at Slade. "I'll get the CSIS jet here and get them onboard before we start to debrief them." They had sent the jet to another airport so Petrov wouldn't see it and ruin their surprise.

"I will clean up here with the local authorities and join you on the plane later. It`s good that we notified them ahead of time that we were operating on US soil with this many dead. I might need input from CSIS to control the scene, although being on a joint task force, we should be able to handle most of it. You can start the debriefing after the girls get settled down some, but we need to do it tonight while everything is still fresh in their minds. They will have heard or seen information we need." Slade went over and hugged both girls in his strong arms.

"You are safe now. Go with Catherine and try to relax. You will be with your mother soon. You can even call her from the plane."

"Thank you," they both said as Catherine took them to the rented CSIS vehicle that had been brought around to wait for the jet.

Barb was pacing the floors of Catherine's home when the door opened and there were her girls, safe and sound. Tears poured down their faces as they hugged each other, reassuring each other that all was well. They were safe and home together.

"Thank you, Catherine. I don't know what I would have done without you and Detective Slade in all of this mess. I can't express my gratitude. It's just too much." Barb was trying to get herself under control for the girls' sake.

"It's fine, Barb. They are safe, and we will keep them safe until this is solved and Sameer is in custody. Go be with them while I make us some tea and then we can talk."

Catherine knew she had to get as much information as she could from the girls while their minds were so focused on their ordeal. She had already debriefed them on the plane, but getting them to talk about it to their mother might bring out more details again. She made the tea and carried the tray into the living room setting it on the coffee table.

She had turned on a listening device on her phone to record their statements and sat that on the coffee table as well. She wanted them to feel safe telling their mother everything that had happened and she knew it would all come out as a jumble of words so the recording would be very useful to sort it all into information she could use.

"Have some tea, ladies. Here, let me pour you some." Catherine poured tea in four cups and sat back on the chair. "I am going to record our conversation on my phone. OK? Just start from the beginning of your day. What did you do in the morning? I know you share an apartment on campus. Were you heading to class? Did you leave together?"

"We got up, ate some breakfast. I put my dishes in the dishwasher. Kara put hers in the sink. I don't know why you do that when you could just as easlly put them in the dishwasher. Never mind. That's not important. Then we left for our first class at Timmins Hall at ten o'clock. We were walking up University Avenue when a black SUV pulled up and three men got out and grabbed us and put us in the car. They had guns! It was really scary!" Sarah's voice broke.

"You are doing very well, Sarah. Were they the same men who took you to the airfield today?"

"No, they were Sameer's men and they stayed at the warehouse."

"Ok, keep going. Do you know where they took you?" asked Catherine.

"No, they shoved us in the back seat and told us not to look up, to keep our heads down on our knees."

"Did you hear any distinct sounds?"

"Yes, I heard bells chiming," said Sarah.

"How long after you were put in the car did you hear them?" asked Catherine.

"About ten minutes, maybe. We were so scared!"

"Ok, you are doing very well. Do you know where they took you? Did you see the street or number?"

"It was a warehouse. I could smell the ocean and hear ships horns and they drove the car into the building so we couldn't see the street," said Sarah.

"How many men were there?"

"At least twenty," she replied.

"There were twenty-three." Kara spoke for the first time.

"Thank you, Kara."

Kara was a watcher, much quieter than her twin sister, but also more observant. Sarah was much more extraverted, livelier, more outgoing.

"Did either of you notice anything particular about the men?" Catherine was watching them closely.

"Just that they weren't all friendly with each other. It seemed that there were two groups of men. They even spoke different languages; six spoke Arabic, the rest spoke Russian. The Russians could all speak English, but not all the Arabs could speak it. One man who seemed in charge of them, the Arabs, didn't like the Russian man. He was arguing with him about money. He was supposed to have it and if he didn't get it soon all their plans would fail. And that wasn't an option. That's what he said, "Failure is not an option, we fail, we die" in a really scary voice."

Sarah was majoring in linguistics and she knew some Arabic and Russian.

"Did they say a name? Talk about anyone specifically?" asked Catherine.

"Just that the Arab man was called Sameer and he called the Russian Petrov. Sameer was the mean one." Kara leaned into her mother's arms and Barb hugged her tightly.

"That's great, honey. I am so proud of you both. You both stayed calm, listened. I am so sorry you got dragged into this." Barb was fighting to stay calm in the aftermath of feeling so scared, petrified her girls would be hurt or killed.

"Yes, you both are very smart. I am proud of you, too. Many adults wouldn't have behaved so well. But you are safe now. We won't let him get to you again. You will have to stay here for a few days until your place is ready on the thirtieth floor and then you can move in. Guards will be posted at your door and I am afraid you will be restricted until this is resolved. I will speak to your Dean of Students and explain the circumstances to her so your grades will not be affected. It's almost time for Christmas break and hopefully, this will all be over by the first of the year." Catherine tried to reassure the girls that their lives would soon be back to normal. Better than normal really since their father was gone, thought Catherine. That thought just popped into her head leaving her uneasy for some reason. Ron might be dead, but he was still hurting them.

Just then the doorbell rang. Slade had arrived to interview the girls. Catherine knew he would be kind but thorough as they needed the information the girls had as soon as they could get it. As Catherine took his coat, she looked into his eyes. He put his hand on her shoulder and squeezed gently. She smiled at him and thought, I really trust him. She hadn't had a man in her life for a long time. Maybe it would be nice if it was this one.

As they all settled back in the living room, the girls smiled at him. They trusted him too, which was surprising because the relationship with their father had never let them put their trust in a man. He smiled back. Maybe he was more than just an animal whisperer.

"How are you both doing?" he asked.

"Good," said Kara.

"Better," said Sarah.

They both replied at the same time.

"Thank you for saving us," said Sarah the more outgoing of the two. Kara just smiled at him and nodded.

"You are very welcome. I am sure Catherine has asked you some questions of your ordeal, but I need to ask some, too. Is that alright with you?"

Both girls nodded.

Catherine by Evonne D. Haley

"Can you tell me the names of any of the men who took you?"

"Not the ones who took us in the SUV. When we got to the warehouse, the man named Geb came over and stayed with us. He's the one who talked to us the most. He wasn't too bad. He didn't hit us or anything like the man called Sameer." Sarah answered. "Sameer was the man who ordered everyone around. He was nasty and scary. Even his men were mean, not like the Russian guy and his men."

"What was he like, the Russian guy?" asked Slade.

"He talked to us nicely and kept us away from Sameer and his men. He told Geb to stay with us."

"What did you think of him, Kara?" asked Slade. He knew she was the one who didn't say much, but she watched.

"I think he could be mean, but he wasn't with us," she replied.

149

"Why do you think that?" Slade questioned her softly.

"His men. They weren't afraid of the other men or the man called Sameer. They looked to him, the Russian. His name was Petrov. Sameer was nasty, but he wasn't the boss even if he thought he was. He was yelling and pointing to us and whatever the Russian said to him scared him, Sameer. He backed off. So, I think he was scared of the Russian." Kara explained.

"You have good instincts, Kara." Slade smiled at her.

"Did the Russian tell you where he was taking you?" asked Catherine.

"To Russia," answered Kara. "I heard him telling Geb to make sure the pilot had made the flight plan."

"Did he say why he was taking you to Russia?" questioned Slade.

"Not really; he just said he would keep us safe."

"Is that what he said, `He would keep you safe?' Those words exactly?"

Slade wanted to make sure he had the context right.

"Yes, those words. He told Geb, 'Stay with them and keep them safe until we get on the plane.'

"Ok. Did you hear of any places named where they were staying or going to later?"

"No. I don't think so," Kara said frowning.

"Yes," offered Sarah. "Sameer said they were going back to the townhouse to pack, remember? On Walker Street. But they're not staying there. They were going to the ship called the "Water Walker". I remember because of the two Walkers."

"Oh, I didn't hear that. I was watching the men taking all the guns and those funny grey packages that looked like bricks. They put them into the white van." Kara stated.

"Did you see the license plates on any of the vehicles?" asked Slade quietly. He didn't want to put pressure on the girls but this information could help them capture Sameer and his men.

"I only saw the one they were putting the packages in," answered Kara. "It was HLP 911. I thought that was really funny." She smiled a little. "Maybe they didn't know what it meant. Their English was not very good."

"That`s great, both of you. You have given us a lot of useful information. Now about the men. Did any of them have any scars, tattoos, disfigurements? Does anything stand out about them?" Slade was prompting their memories.

"Geb had a scar down his face from the corner of his eye to his lip on the left side. I don't know his name." Kara's voice was fading. Both girls were getting tired.

"That's great, Kara. How about you, Sarah? Do you remember anything special about the other men?"

"No." Sarah paused.

"What, honey? Do you remember something?" asked her mother.

"No. It's just that Geb seemed familiar to me, but I know I have never met him before. He was the one with the scar on his face. I don't know. I am really tired." Sarah looked exhausted. They all did.

"Yes, and the man named Petrov looked familiar to me, too." Said Kara as she frowned and then yawned.

"Ok, that's all for now. We will talk again tomorrow. Have a good sleep, if you can. They won't get to you again. You are safe now. You have both helped us a lot and I am very proud of you. There will be two of my men outside the door all night and more outside on the street. If you think of anything or you remember something important or even a small detail, write it down and we will talk later. OK? Here is my card." Slade gave one to each of them. "You can call me anytime of the day or night. OK?"

"OK." Both girls said together.

153

"I'll walk you out, Detective," said Catherine as she rose when he did.

When they were outside the doorway, Catherine looked at Slade. "They have helped us a great deal."

"Yes, and more details will come out tomorrow. They are both smart and observant." Slade put on his coat. "Send me a copy of the recording, will you?"

"Sure," said Catherine. "Something bothering you?"

"I am not sure what it is. I'll have to think about it. We will talk in the morning and don't forget about dinner Thursday at seven." Slade smiled at her. They had changed the night of their dinner.

"I'm looking forward to it, Jeremy," she smiled back.

Chapter 21

Petrov stared out of the thirty-fourth-floor window in downtown Toronto. He had recruited Delong to launder the money from the fake NPO websites, the Syrian Way being the largest one. He had worked with him previously for his own purposes. Now he had to deal with his treachery and Sameer`s volatile temper. The money from the websites was to fund weapons for Sameer to buy from him.

Things had not gone well today. He had lost seven good men, loyal men, and he had lost the leverage he had over Barbara Delong. She had police contacts he hadn't known about. The detective in charge of her husband's death was smart and had resources; but it was her lawyer, Catherine Henley, who had really surprised him. She was a CSIS agent, not a lawyer.

Her resources included tapping into his communications. That was the only way they could have known exactly where and when he would be at the airport in New York with the girls. Unless he had a mole. Or Sameer did. That was disturbing in so many ways. Now he had to not only replace his men, but he had to deal with Sameer's complaints concerning another of Petrov's failures. He was getting a little fed up with Sameer and his mouth.

Barbara Delong had really surprised him. She was so much stronger than he had thought she would be. This woman had depths of intelligence and cunning. If she knew where the money was, and he didn't know that yet, she had made an unexpected move by bringing in the TOPD and the CSIS. This made him think she didn't have the money, because who would want them investigating what you were trying to hide. Yet, with her contacts she would know what they knew all the time. He decided then to get closer to her. The girls would be protected and guarded well so that he couldn't use them as leverage any longer. Now he would have to go directly to Barb and find her other weaknesses, if she had any. He had resources as well and he would now have to start using them.

Sameer was angry, furious. He had killed the two men on the surveillance team and captured the twins, and then Petrov had foiled him. He was no closer to the money than he had been before. Petrov was soft, caring for those girls when they were expendable. He should have killed them and sent their bodies back to the mother one piece at a time. Then she would have told him where the money was. Sameer needed that money. His leader would have no problem excising his body parts to get what he wanted and he would do it out of spite, just to make a statement to others like him.

Sameer would have to take matters into his own hands to get the money. He might not be able to get close to the girls again soon; they would be closely guarded at all times now. He did know, however, where the mother worked and there would be lots of places to take her. She would not keep her secrets from him for long.

Catherine by Evonne D. Haley

Chapter 22

Slade was at his desk the next morning early when Catherine walked in smiling.

"Good morning, Catherine. You seem very chipper today." Slade greeted her.

"Good morning to you too. I have something for you." She opened her hand and passed him an evidence bag with the key Ella had brought to her this morning.

"Is that what I think it is?"

"I think so. Ella found it in the Chinese puzzle box Barb gave her when she helped her move to my place. It was Ron's. I am working on a subpoena to gain access to his safety deposit box at the bank this morning. Barb didn't know he had a second one other than the one they both used. So, yes, I am hopeful this could be what we need to crack this case open." Catherine was all smiles as her phone rang. "Great timing. The subpoena's ready. Coming with me?" she was teasing him.

"Ok, let's pick up the subpoena and see what's in the box." Slade smiled too. Finally, information was coming in. With what the girls had told him and what was, hopefully, in the deposit box, they might be able to move on both Sameer and Petrov.

Twenty minutes later they entered the bank, spoke to the manager and were given the box. The manager then left them alone with it in an empty room. Catherine watched Slade open the box. She stood beside it with her hand on his shoulder. Inside was a book, a ledger with numbers in it.

"What does it all mean?" she asked him.

"I am not sure," he replied as he turned the pages trying to get a sense of their meaning.

"None of the figures are over ten thousand. I think these are the money transfers. There is a lot of money here. Let`s go talk to the manager again. I want to see if these were sent from this bank."

The manager had not gone far. He knew when the TOPD and CSIS came in with a subpoena there would be more questions. He took them to his office and brought up a second account of Delong's on his computer. Barb didn't know about that either. As he looked at the book Slade passed to him, he could see by the corresponding letters to the dollar figures that some came from his bank.

"We will need a printout of every transaction Ron Delong has made from all of his accounts for the past three years, please." Catherine requested.

"Certainly, that is in the subpoena parameters. I'll get it right away. Be right back." The bank manager was being very co-operative, thought Catherine.

"What do the letter's next to the dollar amounts mean? Are they code for the bank accounts they were transferred to? Hopefully, the bank records will show us where they were transferred." Catherine was leaning over Slade's shoulder reading the ledger.

Slade felt her brush up against his back. It felt so natural for her to do that. It wasn't a sexual touch; it was an intimate one. She belonged there. It felt right.

Later that day in the task force conference room, they found some of the bank accounts where the money was transferred. It was going to take awhile to figure out the maize of shell companies that Ron had set up to hide the money.

He had to have a list of them and their account numbers somewhere; a legend to go with the money. That was the key they needed to bring this whole financial web down. He must have kept them separate for security, but where would he have hidden it? It wasn't in the townhouse where he lived, or in the apartment on Richmond, and it wasn't on his computer. It had to be somewhere accessible, but where? And that was assuming it was still in those bank accounts.

He had learned a great deal about the man and Slade felt Ron would have been devious enough to have even hidden it in Barb's possession, but she should have found it when she packed up the townhouse if it had been there and if she had recognized it for what it was. That was the problem. It could be on a memory stick, on a piece of paper in a book, hidden behind a photo, anywhere.

While Catherine worked on the money laundering side of the joint case, Slade worked on Ron's murder. Forensics from the crime scene had listed a man's footprint in the blood on the ground. It was a special print, because it was the cast of a very expensive Italian shoe that had the logo of the maker on the sole. Slade would bet his paycheck it belonged to Petrov. His search into the man showed he was meticulous about his appearance and always looked dressed to the nines and was always seen in the elite social circle of Toronto's high society with a beautiful woman on his arm. Maybe that is where Kara had seen him; in the Toronto newspaper. He made a note to ask her.

Slade put the two computer gurus on the task force, Sam and Craig, to work to find out if Petrov had bought the expensive leather shoes. If he did, Slade could get a subpoena to search his residence and person. It wouldn't be enough to convict him, but it would be one more piece of the puzzle.

Petrov's actions with the twins were enough to put him in the limelight of the investigation. Although Slade and his men saw Petrov at the airport, it was dark, and they had no evidence he was there, no pictures and all his men there were dead so they couldn't testify against him. Also, from the girls' statements he could say he was trying to keep them safe. Slade was still pondering that one. Why would Petrov tell them he was going to keep them safe? Safe from Sameer? Was he working with Sameer or was he a separate element altogether? Was he working for himself or someone else? Something told Slade that he needed to answer these questions.

Slade needed evidence, direct evidence, the smoking gun or a confession would do.

The shoe cast was still just part of the circumstantial evidence, but even that was starting to add up. Slade was sure Petrov would be very careful of his actions now, too. Maybe they could lure him with the money Ron had hidden. There were several ways they could do it, but he didn't want to use Barbara. She and her girls had been through enough. Slade would have to think on this.

Catherine by Evonne D. Haley

Chapter 23

Maggie waited at the restaurant for Ella and Catherine to have dinner that night. They kept this appointment at least once a month, planned around it, the third Wednesday of every month. Only an emergency prevented this event. They all needed to unwind, catch up with one another, knowing they had the unswerving loyalty of their friends, of each other.

She waved from her seat as she saw them come in. They always reserved this table. It was secluded, stuck in a corner at the back where they wouldn't be overheard.

They all hugged and greeted each other laughing, just happy to see one another.

"It's so good to see you guys," exclaimed Catherine. "I have really missed you."

"Me, too," Maggie and Ella both said at once. They all grinned and took their seats in the round corner booth.

Catherine by Evonne D. Haley

The waiter came and took their drink orders and then left them each a menu.

"So. How are the families?" Catherine asked as she placed her napkin on her lap.

"We are good," said Maggie. Her son Corey owned a recording studio and was doing very well with it; business was increasing every quarter. Maggie was so proud of him for living his dream, making it with hard work and the drive to succeed in helping other's dreams come true.

"Corey and Katie are getting married next spring," she announced, smiling.

"That's great, Maggie!" exclaimed Ella. She knew Maggie was hoping for grandchildren someday soon before she was too old to keep up with them. "My girls are great, too. Tanya is applying for grad school next year. There will be changes for sure. Some of the schools are in the States and I will really miss her and so will Bobby."

Bobby, short for Roberta, and her sister, Tanya, had always been close, even though they fought something terrible at times growing up. Although, as they got older they became more tolerant of each other and accepted their differences.

"Anyway, let's hear about Barb. How is she doing after the scare with the girls? And are we still having the house warming for them?" asked Ella.

"Yes, I think we should," answered Catherine. "They are moving this Saturday, so we could have it as a moving/housewarming party. Bring your girls, Ella, if they can make it. We can order in pizza and help them celebrate. They really need to have something positive happen in their lives."

"That sounds great. I will tell the girls," replied Ella. She stared at Catherine, smiling mischievously. "Soooo. How is Detective Slade, Catherine? Seen him lately?"

"Yes, he is fine," she answered her friend blushing slightly as she moved the salt and pepper side by side. "We postponed our meeting until tomorrow night."

"You mean your date, right?" teased Maggie.

"Well, I won't know until we have it." Catherine was very unsure of herself. She hadn't been on a date for a long time, years. "I like him. He is warm, caring, even when questioning Barbara and her girls. He really tries to put them at ease. Most detectives are not that friendly. They just want answers and some even bully to get them. He's not like that. He sympathizes with them and they open up to him. Well, at least the girls do. Barb is still very reserved around him, but it is a very trying time for her and she is naturally reserved around people anyway."

Catherine looked at her two best friends. She was not smiling. "Barb and I have talked a great deal since she came to stay with me. I thought I really knew her, but I didn't know things were so bad between her and Ron until I saw how they lived. That townhouse they shared was sterile almost. Like no one lived there. It had no warmth. You couldn't have guessed that a married couple with two children had ever shared that house together. The Barb I knew when we were younger was so different. I guess after the girls went to college, she just gave up any pretense her and Ron were married at all and she withdrew into herself more and more. I remember thinking when the twins went off to college in the States that she seemed relieved, which was odd. Most mothers feel sad, even depressed. Psychologists call it the empty nest syndrome. Barb seemed almost happy, like a huge burden was taken from her. Now I know it was because she got the girls away from Ron.

It must have been awful to live in that house. The girls' rooms were bare, no personal items left in them, just the beds and dressers. She never meant for them to move back there. What they didn't take with them, she had packed away and put in storage. Most girls would want to come home on holidays and breaks to see their stuff in their rooms, sort of easing them into becoming independent. These girls had taken all their personal items with them and were independent the day they left for college. Barb set them up in a two-bedroom apartment just off campus. They had definitely left the family home. They never intended to move back to that townhouse. Barb was visiting them there in their apartment." Catherine paused for breath.

"Wow," said Maggie. "I knew the townhouse was uncluttered, almost bare really, but Barb is sort of like that herself. I have often found houses to be mirrors of their owners, and Barb is often reserved and uncluttered herself. There is no chatter in her speech, just quiet answers and polite questions as to your welfare; and if you turn the conversation onto her, she turns it back on others as quickly as she can. I feel badly that I never tried to get closer. Maybe we could have helped her more. Maybe we should have killed that bastard. Someone really did Barb and her girls a favour by shooting him. Oh, that makes me so mad! I am a Christian and here I am glad someone got murdered!" Maggie sat back against the upholstered red booth and sighed agitatedly as her friends burst out laughing.

Catherine by Evonne D. Haley

"I understand, Maggie, how you feel. I feel guilty, too, that I never noticed how bad thing were. Barbara is my friend and I didn't do anything to help her even though I knew things weren't good between her and Ron. She never said anything to me, but I knew by what she didn't say. She never talked about him at all, just the girls. So, because she wasn't complaining, I never asked. She probably wouldn't have taken my help, because she is so private, but I should have told her I was there for her if she needed it. I wouldn't have treated you guys like that." Catherine felt she had failed her friend.

"That's because we complain all the time. We have never kept secrets from each other. I know I was always blubbering on about my woes. You never had to try to pry stuff out of me. I never stopped complaining. You were probably sick of me at times. But still," Ella held up her hand to Catherine. "I depended on you two. You were and still are my anchors in life. I never feel alone. I know I can depend on you to be there for me and my girls, and I thank God for you every day. You have, many, many times helped me get through the trials that come with raising three kids alone while studying and working full time. I couldn't have done it without you. I can't even imagine what Barb's life has been like or her girls'; all those years living with an abusive man must have left scars on them, but they seem to love and care for each other and others as well." Ella sat up straighter. "Well, we will be there for them now. Saturday, we will help them start a new life and show them we are all there for them, as well as just telling them the words. As my Grammy used to say, "The proof is in the pudding!"

"Your grandmother was a wise woman, Ella. I really loved her," smiled Maggie.

"I miss her, too. If I live to be ninety, maybe I will be half as smart as she was," grinned Catherine. Inside she was thinking she had just heard something important, but she laughed with her two friends and let it go.

The waiter returned and took their orders.

Catherine by Evonne D. Haley

"Was the key what you needed?" Ella asked Catherine after he left.

"Yes, it helped a lot. I can't say more, but it was another piece of the puzzle. We will bring them down. The key to Ron's code is still out there. We just need to find it. He would have kept it close so he could access it; it's probably right under our noses. We just need to recognize it for what it is. Enough shop talk. Is it going to be a big wedding?" she asked Maggie.

Catherine watched as Maggie's face became animated as she talked about her son. There was such warmth and life in her eyes. Both of her friends cared about their children, their families, each other, their jobs. They were alive and meeting life's challenges and rewards head on, confident they could celebrate the good times and overcome the bad. All three of them shared Christian beliefs and used their faith in God as a daily compass to guide them. It was also their faith in each other, their confidence they were not alone

that eased the burdens and spread the joy.
She had never seen that look on Barb's face.

Chapter 24

Barbara was working at Catherine's house. She had her phone, her computer and a fax machine. The only difference in her daily routine was that she had to reschedule her appointments with her clients. She called them all personally to reassure them that everything was fine, their money was still in good hands, nothing had changed with Ron's death. She just needed a few days to handle personal affairs. Most understood and had faith in her, in the firm. Some were fearful and needed a lot of reassurance, which she provided. She would lose some, but it wouldn't cripple the firm. That out of the way, Barb started on Ron's list of new clients. Everything looked good on paper, but when she tried to contact them personally by phone, she ran into problems.

Some contact information led to messenger companies that passed on the inquiries to their clients, who never responded. She assumed the messages had previously gone to Ron. When she tried to e-mail them, the same thing happened. Ron had set these fake clients up with contact information that came to him, so he could deflect any inquiries.

Barb had allowed Ron too much leeway. It had all looked good on paper, even legitimate addresses for them. But they were all fake and there were twenty-one of them. What was he using them for? It certainly wasn't for building her company. He had had enough real customers to justify his salary, so why did he need fake ones? It must have taken a long time to set them up as shell companies of shell companies many layers thick. It would take a great deal of time and effort to follow the paper trail to its fake conclusion.

Barb was looking for a common name for all of them. That name would connect Ron to Petrov or Sameer. She was sure of it. Detective Slade and Catherine were working on this, too; but Barb had the advantage, because she knew Ron and he had let his ego reign over his common sense. He had left clues in the fake names and addresses of the companies he had set up. Some of the companies were real ones with a letter missing or inserted in the name and included the real address with one number off. Anyone looking at these companies would just think it was a typo and once they verified it was a legitimate company, would move onto the next name on the list. They would have to work deeper to see the error.

Barb started a spreadsheet and entered the twenty-one names. Then she laboriously broke down the shell companies of each one. Two thirds of the way down she saw the pattern. She couldn't believe her eyes. Ron had used the firm's legitimate clients to funnel money through contributions to his fake companies supposedly for aid overseas to refugees in the Middle East. The money from these companies all funneled into one non-profit company, the Syrian Way. Ron must have planned this for years. It would have taken a lot of time to set this all up. When tax time came in February, there would be no tax receipts from these fake companies for her firm's established clients.

This would ruin her company. And her. And that changed everything.

Chapter 25

Catherine was putting on her earrings when the doorbell rang. Slade was right on time.

"Hello, Slade. Come in," she greeted him with a smile.

"You can call me Jeremy, if you like," he returned her smile. "Wow! You look lovely. That blue dress is wonderful on you. It brings the blue out in your eyes."

"Thank you, Jeremy." Catherine felt her face flush at the compliment. "I'm ready. Where are we going?"

"I have a reservation at a little restaurant down in China Town. It's owned by a friend of mine and the food is great." Slade helped her put her coat on and squeezed her shoulders lightly.

Catherine felt a little shy, which was unusual as she was a confident woman at the worst of times. She hadn't been out on a date for several years. Slade was nervous as well,

181

but his was caused by his wanting to make a good impression on Catherine. Working on the cases revealed their professional personalities, their ethics and their abilities to work with a team. Being on a date could show them their more personal sides, their sense of humor, and their softer sides that included their attraction to each other. Or not.

In the car on their way to the restaurant they agreed not to talk about the case. This was a get-to-know you outing, not a staff meeting. At the restaurant, the owner greeted Jeremy with smiles and a big hug. He was loved here for saving their son from a life of crime and eventual imprisonment or death.

After being served wine and deciding on their meals, Jeremy sat back and watched Catherine. She had been charming to the waiter as well as the owner. Now she sat back in her chair, relaxed and smiling at him.

"This is a nice spot. If the food is as good as it sounds, I will be coming back here." She said.

Catherine by Evonne D. Haley

"It is one of my favourite places to eat," agreed Jeremy smiling back at her.

As the evening progressed their conversation went from their backgrounds, parents, books, movies, to their future plans and dreams. Both were relaxed, enjoying each other's company. The food was delicious, the atmosphere congenial; and as they learned more about each other, they found commonalities as well as contrasts, which kept their interest's piqued.

Jeremy told her about his parents, both still living in the suburbs of Toronto, and his brother, who was a military man based in the Middle East. He was in intelligence so not a lot of details about him, but she got the impression they were close. Slade had been in the air force also in intelligence, but was honorably discharged after being wounded. He came home and applied to the TOPD. With his history, he had no problem getting in. He enjoyed his work, but didn't have much of a social life due to the long hours he put in. And maybe, he had been waiting for her, he thought suddenly.

Catherine understood the long hours and less than active social life. Her upbringing was similar to Jeremy's, except she was an only child and her parents were both deceased. Her family was Ella and Maggie and their families.

She had been employed by CSIS right out of university due to her high scores on aptitude tests and her ability to speak five languages. She had completed her doctorate in International Law and then under the umbrella of CSIS, she had graduated with a doctorate in Linguistics and Middle East Studies. She loved her work. She felt she was making a difference in righting the world of evil, although sometimes it felt like she was going backwards when information was slow coming in and criminals walked. For now.

Jeremy found Catherine interesting, as well as beautiful. He could see and hear her love for her friends, the trust she had in them. They also shared the spiritual belief in God, how He kept them grounded in their jobs and uplifted in their faith that good would overcome evil in this world someday. Until then, they did their jobs, thanked God for all the wonderful people in their lives and prayed for those who weren't so wonderful.

Leaving the restaurant, Jeremy took her hand casually in his as they walked to the car. Catherine kept it there, liking the feeling of intimacy between them. When he opened her door, he stopped her from getting in the car and put his hands on her shoulders. She looked up at him knowing he was going to kiss her. When his lips brushed against hers, she put her hands on his chest, but not to push him away. Her fingers clutched his lapels and pulled him closer. At her insistence, he deepened the kiss. Enfolding her in his arms, he lifted her up to his chest. She was tiny compared to him; but she fit perfectly there, like she belonged. His. When he pulled his lips from hers, she slowly opened her eyes looking straight into his and smiled. He smiled back.

Catherine by Evonne D. Haley

"That went well," she said.

"Didn't it though. But maybe we should practice more just to make sure," he grinned at her like a little boy who was wheedling his way into another cookie.

"Maybe, but not tonight. I have an early meeting in the morning and so do you." She wiggled a little for him to put her down.

"I wouldn't do that, if you want me to let you go, Catherine." Now his grin was a fake leer.

Laughing she said, "Stop that and put me down, lover boy."

Still grinning he let her go and helped her into the car.

"I can wait." He smiled as he closed her door. She was worth waiting for.

Catherine hoped he wouldn't wait too long.

The meeting the next morning at the task force conference room started at seven a.m.

with reports from each of the teams working on the different areas of investigation. Slade brought everyone up-to-date on the evidence collected on the murder investigation. Catherine reported on the information from the girls on their abduction. Craig and Sam gave a power point presentation of material found on Ron's computer similar to what Barb had figured out on her own. Fran and Helen showed how the money was moved around from the book found in the safety deposit box. Finally, Marianne and Ren summed it all up in a presentation that included what could happen next based on what had already occurred.

Although this was unusual in an investigation normally based solely on evidence, Catherine and Slade both felt it was an invaluable part of the investigation. It gave them an insight into the events being played out, what the players might do next based on what was known of them and their activities. The one thing they didn't know was what Sameer's agenda was, what or who his target was and who was really calling the shots.

Sameer was too volatile to be in charge. Also from the twins' statement, Sameer was afraid of Petrov or who Petrov knew.

This was interesting because Petrov was Russian and there were hints of a Russian influence in terrorist activities in Iran. Although Petrov hadn't been connected to Iran before, he was now. Also, the fact he wasn't afraid of Sameer showed either he was an idiot or he was connected to the people who controlled Sameer. And no one thought Petrov was an idiot.

What really intrigued Slade was the fact that Petrov had attempted to take the girls to Russia to keep them safe. Why? What did the girls mean to Petrov? Or was he trying to keep them safe from Sameer who wouldn't think anything of killing them? Again why? Was he using them to get to Barb? Did he really believe she knew where the money was? And again, why would he believe that?

Catherine was pondering the same questions and not feeling good about it. It also brought back the memory of Kara telling her that she thought Petrov looked familiar; and although he had been in the newspaper in the society section several times, Kara didn't think she had seen him there. Still, that could be why she thought he was familiar, even if she didn't remember the photo. Catherine made a note to talk to her again.

"Ok, folks. Things are moving along," said Slade. "Craig and Sam, continue breaking down Ron's computer files. Fran and Helen, you need to continue following the money trail. There is an end to it, hopefully, where someone has actually placed their hands on it. Marianne and Ren, I want you to go back through any, and all information on Petrov as far back as his conception. There is something there, some connection we are not seeing. I get the feeling Sameer is expendable, but Petrov isn't. Look at his associates and past business dealings. Find out where he and Delong met up, any common friends, acquaintances, business partners, clients, events they have both attended, anything and everybody who could have connected them.

Roger, would you please get Jenny and some of the support staff to put everything we now know into chronological order; information and events both. I know this is Friday, but we need to continue working through the weekend. Anyone who wants to attend religious services on Saturday or Sunday can come in after. Just let Roger know. I wouldn't ask this of you, but time is a factor; lives are at stake and not just the Delong women's. We don't know what Sameer's objectives are. It could be thousands of lives at risk, and we don't know their time table. Petrov isn't the only potential arms dealer Sameer could be using. He could go around him, if his goal is time stamped or he loses trust in Petrov. We need to know this a.s.a.p. Also, Sameer is a zealot and very unpredictable. We have people watching him, but more information is needed before he gives us the slip or acts on his own.

I want to thank you for all your hard work. You are bringing us closer with each and every piece of information you are uncovering." Slade was proud of the team he and Catherine had put together. They were some of the best minds in both the TOPD and CSIS and they worked unceasingly, focused totally on bringing these men to justice.

Everyone filed out of the room except Catherine and Slade.

"We don't know nearly enough yet," said Catherine.

"No, but I meant what I said to the others. Every piece of information is bringing us closer. It's like a puzzle. Each piece fits into the picture. We just need more pieces. They are great agents, smart, intuitive, the best in their fields."

"I know. I keep thinking I am missing something. Something right in front of me and I am a little frustrated." Catherine frowned.

"Well, Roger is going to have the report I requested the day after tomorrow. Maybe that will trigger something in your memory. Why don't you take tomorrow off? You have been working more hours than all of us combined. You need a break."

"I think I will take you up on that. I will help Barb and her girls move into their new home tomorrow. Maggie and Ella are helping too. We want to make it a fun day for them, a new beginning." Catherine was frowning. "There's that feeling again. I just can't figure why I get it when I think of their moving. Oh, that's so frustrating!"

Slade came closer to her. "Maybe you need something to take your mind off it, to give it a rest. That's usually when you remember what you were looking for." He put his arms around her and gave her a hug, but didn't release her right away

"That's not helping, Jeremy," she was grinning. "It's just making my mind go blank!"

"Really? That's good, isn't it? Tell me that's good, Cat." He commanded hugging her tighter.

"It's very good, Slade. It's just not what we should be doing if someone walks in." She stepped out of his arms and then leaned in and gave him a slow kiss on his lips. She left the room laughing over her shoulder, "Later, lover boy."

Slade stood there grinning. He really loved her sense of humor.

Chapter 26

"Well, that's the last box, except the one marked Personal, Do Not Open; that one I put in your room, Barb. You are all officially moved in, ladies," announced Catherine.

All seven ladies high-fived each other.

"Let's break in that new sectional and that huge flat screen TV. I brought some popcorn and a few movies. They're in my bag by the front door." Catherine told the four young girls, Kara, Sarah, Tanya and Bobby as they ran to find the bag. Their mothers had terrible taste in movies, so they would pick it. Catherine usually had good taste in movies so they should have some good ones in the bag to choose from.

"Thank you, so much, all of you," Barb sighed. She had looked terribly tired and stressed that morning, but seemed better now, tired but not so stressed. This move was a big step for Barb and her girls; the first one into their future.

"Hey, I just wanted a day off," laughed Catherine.

"I came for the pizza," Maggie said, as she looked into the box on the counter. "Oh, it's all gone. Rats."

"I'll order in some good food from Roberto's down the street as a thank you for all the help you have given me and the girls today and every day since this all began. I don't know what I would have done without you!" Barb wiped away a tear on her cheek. "How many times have I said that? You all must be so sick of me and my problems!"

Catherine went over and hugged her. "You are a very strong woman, Barb. Give yourself some credit. You have handled all of this better than I would have. Now, you have moved into your fabulous new home, the girls are safe here with you, and this case will be wrapped up soon. We are getting closer every day."

Barb hugged her back.

"What movie did you girls pick?" asked Ella as they came back into the room giggling.

"Spy!" they all said at once.

"I love that movie!" exclaimed Catherine as they all picked seats on the sectional. It was a tight squeeze, but all seven of them got comfortable. Max counted as the eighth as she settled on Barb's lap.

"Who's going to put the movie in?" asked Ella.

They looked at each other and started laughing. Barb sat back and smiled. This was what it was supposed to be like in your own home, laughing with family and friends.

Halfway through the movie, Catherine's phone started vibrating in her pocket. She stood up.

"Keep going. I'll be right back," she said as she left the room.

"I'm sorry to interrupt moving day, but something has come up and you should be here." Slade stated in a tight voice.

"Ok, I'm on my way," responded Catherine immediately heading for the door and closing her phone. Slade would never have called if it wasn't something important.

"Sorry, ladies, but I have to leave. We will do this again soon. Have a great night."

Sarah paused the movie and they all hugged her goodbye.

"I'll see you again soon, Max," Catherine hugged the tiny Yorkie. "Call me if you need me, Barb."

"Thanks for everything, Catherine," Barb said taking Max back into her arms.

Chapter 27

When Catherine entered the conference room, the place was buzzing.

"What's going on?" she asked Slade.

"We found Sameer, dead. We don't have a positive ID on him yet; he was shot in the back of the head, not pretty coming out the front, not much left of his face. The men watching him lost him in the subway late last night. Two patrolmen found him in an alley downtown on the waterfront, after we received an anonymous tip of a dead body. The tipster had a Russian accent. You can hear the call yourself to see if you recognize it as Petrov's. I couldn't say for sure as I only heard him speaking once at the airport."

"So, what does this mean on the threat level for the City? Will someone else take his place? Where are his men? Who was next in line to him? Who is second in command? These cells are usually tiered so when one goes the next one gets to be top dog. Do we know who that is and where he is?" Catherine had so many questions she needed answered. She looked over at the task force working on their phones and computers. They all looked tired and pumped at the same time.

"We will have a report in fifteen minutes from Marianne and Ren. Roger has had them all working together on those questions since six this morning." Slade ran his hand over his face; it was now seven-thirty in the evening. He had been here since he received notice of Sameer's murder at five-thirty this morning. He hadn't called Catherine until they had some confirmed information, as he knew she needed the day off from the stress of this case. His phone buzzed on the conference table.

"Yes," his response was clipped showing his fatigue. He listened without speaking for a minute and then said, "We'll be right there. Tell them not to touch anything and that means the van. It could be booby trapped."

"What's happened?" asked Catherine.

"They found the van Sarah told us about with the license plate HLP 911 on the docks. Let's go."

When Catherine and Slade arrived, they saw the area had been cordoned off with police tape to a perimeter of two hundred feet and a uniformed officer came over with the bomb technician, Sydney.

"Glad you're here, Slade. You, too, Catherine. You were right. It is wired to blow, big time; enough C4 in there to take down a building. We put mirrors under the back of the van and saw the explosives that would have gone `boom` if we had opened the doors. That's all we did. We were waiting on you."

"Ok, Sydney. What's your call? Is anyone in the van? Can we see into it without opening the doors?"

"Yes, I have the robot ready with a camera to get close enough to see into the front windshield. The rest of the windows are blacked out with black paint."

"Ok, whenever you're ready. Sergeant Carter, get everyone back out to four hundred feet." Slade ordered.

"I would say five hundred feet would be better. There's a lot of C4 in there," suggested Sydney.

"You heard him, make a perimeter of five hundred feet," said Carter as he extended the crime scene tape out from the van.

Sydney moved the robot in closer to the van with the video feed already recording. He held the controller, watching the view finder and the robot as it zoomed in on the windshield of the van. He moved the toggle switch on the controller to bring the robot in close to the front of the van, but not close enough to touch it. Then he zoomed the camera lens in to get as close as he could to see inside the van.

Slade and Catherine stood at his shoulder staring at the view screen. Inside they could see bodies. Dead bodies, five of them. Sydney took pictures to enlarge later for facial recognition. They could also see wires connected to more bricks of C4 in the back of the vehicle.

"What do you think, Sydney? Can you deactivate the bomb?" asked Slade.

"Yes, I think so. I just need a closer view of the back of the van." He toggled the robot to go to the back of the van and then zoomed in to see under the van without touching it.

"Well, well. That's odd." Sydney was frowning as he took still pictures.

"What?" asked Catherine.

"The wires are not connected to the detonator." Sydney was very nervous.

"Are you sure?"

"Yes, see the wires that are in the C4 come out of the back of the van, but they are not connected to the detonator."

"Get some extreme close ups, Sydney. We don't want to be wrong about this." cautioned Slade.

"Could it be a trap?" Catherine was worried. She didn't want anyone else to lose their lives over this.

"Yes, that is why this will be a slow job. Right, Sydney?"

"Yes, sir. This will take a while. I'll not risk anyone on a hunch or a maybe." Sydney took his job very seriously. He had to. On the front lines, he would be the first person to die.

Two hours later the van had been cleared. Whoever set up this scenario didn't intend to blow anyone up, which was a question in itself. Why? Did they want the police to find the five terrorists intact, for recognition purposes? The twins would be able to identify them. Was this their entire cell? Was the terrorist threat to the City dissolved? Was Petrov behind all of this? If yes, why did he want them identified? Maybe to throw the police off, so they would stop investigating him?

Catherine felt that if they could understand the reason why, they would find out the answers to all the other questions. Someone had done them a favour by eliminating Sameer and his cell as a threat to the city, but why? Was Petrov cleaning house? Not many would take out a terrorist cell unless they were suicidal. Terrorists were into violence and retribution. If it was Petrov's work he had better watch his back from now on. Terrorists also had long memories and were very patient. They could wait years to retaliate.

Slade couldn't help but remember what the twins had told him, that Petrov was in charge, not Sameer, that Sameer's men were afraid of Petrov. The real question now was who was Petrov afraid of?

Back at CSIS in the conference room, the task force was already identifying the five dead terrorists from the international data base with photos taken from the van by the robot.

The team had also found the freighter, Water Walker. It was in international waters heading home, out of their jurisdiction. All chatter had stopped at Sameer's end after the last e-mail from Iran asking if they were coming home for the uncle's funeral. There had been no reply. For good reason; they were apparently all dead.

The task force still didn't have enough information about all the players, especially Petrov.

Catherine had listened to the recording of the call that had tipped Slade that Sameer was dead, but she couldn't verify the voice was Petrov's. Marianne and Ren were still building a portfolio on him. They would be very thorough. Hopefully, they would have a preliminary report within a few more hours.

■■■

Slade's cell phone rang.

"Hi, Patricia. What do you have for me?"

The coroner said, "Slade, I think you should come down here. I have found something unusual in Delong's blood work and bring Catherine."

"On our way," Slade responded as he turned to Catherine. "You should come with me, Catherine. Our coroner has some news on Delong and she wants you there, too."

"Ok," she responded. "Isn't it a bit late to be getting news from the coroner? Ron's been buried for weeks."

"Don't ask me. She says come and I obey." Slade laughed.

Twenty minutes later he and Catherine pushed through the double doors of the coroner's domain.

"What do you have, Pat?"

"What, no hello or a hug?" Patricia asked as she stood with her hands on her ample hips.

"Hello, Patricia," Slade said as he hugged the robust woman.

"Now, that's better." She patted his arm and turned to her desk. "Ok. When I performed Delong's autopsy, I noticed his thyroid had been removed so I took some additional blood tests. They came back with some unusual results. It's taken me all this time to get some answers. He had thyroid cancer caused by exposure to radioactive isotopes, specifically Iodine-131, which was still in his blood. Residual traces can be found in the blood up to thirty years later. These levels of radioactive isotopes are found in one place, Chernobyl. He was exposed to it in 1986 in the Ukraine as a child of fifteen and treated for cancer of the thyroid at the age of twenty-one."

"Wow! That I wasn't expecting." Said Slade

"And there's more. He was treated for it in Russia. Their scientists kept exact records of the effects of the Chernobyl disaster on the children exposed to radioactive isotopes specifically iodine-131 and caesium-137."

"That is interesting. So, who is our Ron Delong?"

"Hold on. This is where it becomes even more interesting. I compared his DNA to their data base and came up with two hits. Delong's DNA matched that of Alexi Petrov."

"And the second hit?" asked Catherine.

"When I saw the residual isotopes in his blood, I spoke with a thyroidologist in Belinsk that I know personally. He remembered the two cases. The second hit wasn't a perfect match but was close. It was for his brother, Pyotr Petrov, who was successfully treated for leukemia caused by caesium-137. They were born in Pripyat, Ukraine; their parents were two of the thirty people immediately killed in the explosion at Chernobyl."

Patricia had just given them a lot of information that could break the case wide open.

"Well, that cannot be just a coincidence. Is Petrov a common name in Russia? Pyotr is Russian for Peter and that is common. Who are our Peter and Alexi Petrov? When did they come to the US and Canada? So many new questions. Alright, I need that report from Marianne and Ren immediately on our Peter Petrov and to get them researching Alexi Petrov. "

"Thank you, Patricia, for your unwavering curiosity and doggedness in running down abnormalities! You've helped us enormously. I don't know how this will play out yet, but I will let you know when I do." Slade patted her shoulder.

"There are more questions now than before," said Catherine as they left the building. Slade just nodded his head.

■■■

Barb Delong sat her desk in her office thinking. Max was sitting on her lap. If she was a cat, she would be purring as Barb stroked her little head. Barb was so worried. How was she to get out of this mess? What could she tell her clients so they wouldn't take what was left of their money and run to another financial consultants' firm and then sue her firm? She could guarantee some of the funds lost but certainly not all that Ron had stolen without bankrupting her firm and herself.

She had to find the money. She needed the banking codes and the account numbers where he had stashed it. Or he might have withdrawn the money and taken it out of the country somehow, though that would be difficult to do. Otherwise, it would have shown up in any of the bank records in Canada or the US. Where was his passport? That would tell her when and where he had traveled recently. Did the police have it? She didn't know, but they could always check with immigration to see where he had been. Maybe Catherine would tell her, if she asked. But she didn't want her to know what was happening at the firm yet. She would know soon enough.

Chapter 28

Slade's cell phone rang just as they were getting into his car.

"Slade, it's John. A woman just showed up at the Delong apartment on Richmond Street. I have sent you her picture."

John and his team were watching from across the hall in an empty apartment. They had installed a hidden camera in Delong's apartment so they could see who entered and what they were doing in it.

"Thanks, John. Stay there and I will get back to you in a minute."

"What now?" asked Catherine as she sat beside Slade in his car.

"That was John. He just sent me a picture of Delong's girlfriend. Well, well. Look who it is." He held out his phone for Catherine to see. "It's J.J. from Delong's office."

"What do you want to do? Do you want to bring her in for questioning?" Catherine asked him.

"No," he replied. "I want to see what she will do and where she will go before she knows we are onto her relationship with Ron." Slade punched numbers into his phone. "Ok, John. Put a tail on her. Keep me informed."

He punched in more numbers. "Marianne, I want you to find out everything you can about Jean Jones. She works at Carter and Delong, Inc. as the receptionist. Get everything you can on her background and her financials. Check her passport, see where she has been traveling the last few years, when she cut her first tooth. Everything there is to find about her. Oh, and compare her passport to Delong's. See if their trips match." Slade hung up and turned to Catherine.

"Maybe we will know something about someone now. We've been running in circles, chasing clues, but not getting anywhere, because no one is who they seem to be."

"Don't get your hopes up yet. I have the feeling we will be searching longer before we know all the players. At least, we have

Sameer out of the picture, although that is in itself a big question. Who took him out and why?"

"We just keep getting more questions. I would like to know some of the answers." Catherine fastened her seat belt as they headed back to the task force conference room.

As Catherine and Slade stepped off the elevator, her boss motioned them both into his office. He was wearing his stern, political face. Two men wearing black suits were also there. Both stood as they entered the room.

"Catherine, this is Agent Carson of the USA's Homeland Security and Agent Johnson from the CIA. Gentlemen, this is Catherine Henley, CSIS, and Jeremy Slade from the TOPD. They are heading our joint task force on an active terrorist cell in Toronto and the related murder of a financial consultant, who we believe was funneling money to support the cell." Both men nodded stoically, silently.

"Agent Johnson, perhaps you can fill us in on your reason for being here." Blanchette took his seat behind his desk and motioned them all to sit.

"Well, Director Blanchette, we are investigating a terrorist cell led by an Iranian named, Sameer, that we believe is planning an attack on the US… …."

"Let me stop you there, Agent Johnson. Sameer and his cell have been eliminated. We found their bodies this morning. We believed they were planning an attack here in Toronto as well. We also believe their money was being funnelled to them here in the city by a financial consultant named Ron Delong." Director Blanchette informed them.

Catherine and Slade looked at each other covertly and then away keeping stoic faces.

Blanchette continued, "Our joint task force is investigating the connection between the murder of Ron Delong and Sameer. We believe Delong was funnelling money through a website called the Syrian Way. The money, however, has disappeared. We are still looking for it. We are also interested in a Russian named Peter Petrov, who we believe is involved with Sameer. Now we have brought you up-to-date, tell us about your investigation. Sameer had five men with him here in Toronto. Do you have reason to believe there are more in the cell?"

Agent Johnson looked at Agent Carson and then said to Director Blanchette, "We are watching a group in the US that we believe is with Sameer and his group, but they disappeared last week. We have photos of them that we can compare to Sameer and his people here." He opened his briefcase and took out some pictures. As he passed them to Blanchette, he continued, "We have heard chatter that they are on their way back to Iran, but we cannot confirm it. Our source on the street has disappeared as well."

Blanchette glanced at the pictures and then passed them to Catherine and Slade.

"These are the men in the van, Sameer's men," confirmed Slade.

Johnson passed him another photo. Slade nodded, "Yes, this is Sameer. He was murdered around three this morning in an ally downtown near the docks."

Johnson nodded. "Ok, that's all the men we know of in the cell. This Petrov, do you have a photo of him?"

"Certainly," said Catherine. She went behind her boss's desk and when he nodded, she tapped a few keys and brought up some of the surveillance photos of Petrov and those she had taken at the funeral. Then she turned the screen around so the two agents could see the screen.

Johnson looked at Carson. Whatever passed between them resulted in a decision to end the meeting.

"Thank you, Director Blanchette. Our job is done thanks to you and your team." Both gentlemen stood up to leave.

"Wait," Catherine and Slade both took a step toward them. "Do you know this man?"

"He is not on any of our terrorist lists." Both men moved to the door and left.

Catherine and Slade looked at each other. They knew the men were lying, but why? Why wouldn't they say they knew Petrov? It was obvious they recognized him. Now Petrov was definitely on Catherine's radar as someone to be watched at all times. She looked at her boss.

"Director, we need more info on Petrov. He's not what or who he seems to be and that makes me very nervous. He also could be the one who took out Sameer's entire cell and we need to know why. Plus, he's involved in Delong's murder and the missing funds. We just learned that he is Delong's brother. There is a lot of questions we need answers to."

"Yes, I agree, Catherine. The task force is still operational. Keep me informed." He dismissed them and went back to work. He was uneasy, because there were too many unanswered questions and he didn't like that.

Chapter 29

J.J. walked quickly down the sidewalk, her stiletto heels clicking on the pavement. She knew someone was watching her, but she figured it was the police, not Sameer or Petrov. She could handle the police; they wouldn't kill her, probably. The others would. After all, she had their money. Ron had warned her at the beginning, 'no one can know about you.' So far, no one did. Now, she feared she had made a colossal mistake coming to the apartment. She had made the decision to come regardless of the risk. She needed the fake passports and the two hundred fifty thousand dollars concealed behind the headboard of the bed to get out of the country. Ron had called it their escape plan. She had chartered a private plane to fly her to Costa Rica this morning and from there she would disappear. After all, she had the money to live wherever she wanted. She just had to get to it.

It was not the police following her. It was someone far more dangerous. It was Barb

Delong. She couldn't believe it when she first realized J.J. was involved. She didn't think J.J. had the brains to pull this off, but so far, she had not been a blip on the police radar at all. This trip to the apartment changed all that, but still only showed she had had an affair with Ron not that she was involved in the money scam. But Barb knew better. J.J. had bragged at the office about her trips to Costa Rica, three in the past year. Now Barb knew why she had taken those trips, to move the money around.

The fact that Ron had carried on an affair with her right under Barb's nose didn't upset Barb; she really didn't care about that. It was the fact he had deliberately ruined her firm by taking her clients money. He knew it would ruin her financially, professionally, and personally. She couldn't replace twenty million dollars in two months before the tax receipts were to be issued. She had to get the money back. That was her only hope. Now, that she knew who had it, she knew what she had to do to get it back; whatever it took. She couldn't go to Catherine, because she was working on the side of justice and justice would take too long. Barb was working on the side of survival and she had a deadline.

Peter Petrov was on his way to Barb's office when he spied her trailing behind J.J. Well, well he thought. This is an interesting development. He had met J.J. once with Ron at the apartment on Richmond, but felt she was just a bimbo Ron was using. Why was Barb following J.J.? Could it mean that J.J. had the money or knew where it was? It could also mean Barb knew it and was going for it.

He watched as J.J. went into the apartment building on Richmond and saw Barb duck into a shop across the street.

When J.J. came out of the building, she carried a suitcase and hailed a cab. Barb tried to get one to follow. There were no other cabs in sight, so Peter pulled to the curb, and leaning over opened the passenger door.

"Get in, Barb, quickly before we lose her," he commanded.

Surprisingly, Barb got in and he pulled out into traffic three cars behind the cab.

"She knows where the money is, doesn't she, Barb.

"Yes, I think so. I need it back to save my company, my career and my life. Ron stole a lot of that money from my clients and I have to put it back before tax time. What are you going to do?"

Peter looked at her and then back to the road. "Barb, it's over one hundred million dollars in total. You could go anywhere and live off that forever. Why would you want to put any of it back?"

"I've thought of that, but my girls need me and I couldn't leave them, especially with the stigma that would be forever attached to their name. I must get the twenty million dollars back that Ron stole from the firm. I know where J.J. is headed. We could both get what we want. Twenty million for me and the rest for you. Do we have a deal?" Barb was shaking.

"She's heading for the airport. Where is she going?" Peter demanded. "I can just follow her in. I don't need your information." Eighty million was a good amount of money, but one hundred million was better.

"Are you sure? I know where she is going. What if you lose her?" Barb was pushing him.

"Ok, deal. Now where is she going?"

"She will make a stop first in Costa Rica," Barb gave him part of the destination. It was the only part she knew, but she wouldn't tell him that.

"Why there? What stop? And how do you know that?" he demanded.

"She's been there three times in the last year. She bragged about it at the office. I didn't think anything of it until she quit this morning and told one of the secretaries that she had to go shopping for a new wardrobe for a warmer climate. Then when I followed her,

223

she came to the apartment Ron had rented last year. I knew he must have had a girlfriend and I didn't care; but it was still a surprise it was J.J."

"She's not going to international departures. She's headed to the private airfield." Peter drove directly to a private hanger. "I've my own plane here. Stay in the car and I will try to get her flight plan and we will follow her down south."

Barb thought it over as she sat there waiting for him. He could kill her and get all the money. Why was she trusting him? She was crazy, but she didn't have a choice now.

■■■

John called Slade on his cell. "J.J. is at Pearson Airport and she has chartered a plane, but you will never believe who is tailing her." John didn't even wait for Slade to respond. "It's Petrov and Barb Delong. It looks like they are going to follow her. Petrov has a private plane here, too. Do you want them apprehended?"

"No, not yet. They are going after the money. We will get their flight plan and go after them. I will get back to you in a few minutes." Slade clicked off and turned to Catherine. "Would you like to go on a trip with me?" he asked her.

"Ok, where are we going?" she looked at him in surprise.

He raised one eyebrow at her fast response and grinned at her. "Remind me of this later. Petrov and Barb Delong followed J.J. to the airport. Looks like they are all going on a trip. Do we have access to the CSIS jet to follow them?"

"Yes, it's at Pearson Airport ready at all times. I`ll just get the Director`s approval." She was already moving out the door.

Twenty minutes later, they were on their way to the airport when Ren called with the flight plan of the two planes. "They are all heading to Costa Rica and will arrive there at six tonight. Director Blanchette ordered our pilot to file a flight plan and should be ready when you get there."

"Thanks, Ren." They really had a super task force of very efficient agents. "Costa Rica," he told Catherine as he hung up.

"I have people in Costa Rica, so we will have eyes on them as soon as they land." She looked at her watch. "Around six p.m. tonight?"

"Right," confirmed Slade.

"Our flight won't be far behind as ours is a bigger jet. We might even beat them there."

Forty minutes later Catherine and Slade were winging their way south in the CSIS jet.

"What can she be thinking? Did Petrov force her to go with him? This is so far from Barb's normal behaviour. I pray she is alright, that we can get her back safely. And J.J! I am sure Barb never knew they were having an affair, but even if she did she wouldn't have cared as long as they were discrete and didn't flaunt it in her face, especially at work. What do you think, Slade?" Catherine was really concerned for her friend and totally floored over the events unfolding.

"Catherine, look at me." Slade turned her head toward him by touching her chin. "We don't know what's going on, whether Barb is involved with Petrov, whether she knew about J.J. and Ron, or if she is being coerced by Petrov. When we get there and talk to her, we can go from there. If it counts, I don't believe she is involved with Petrov. However, I also don't know what's going on for sure."

Catherine looked in his eyes and knew he was being honest with her.

"What do you believe is happening?" she asked searchingly.

"I believe something tipped her off to J.J. and Ron and she followed her to the apartment. It's only five blocks from the office. Somewhere she met up with Petrov and they followed her to the airport. We know he has a small private jet there. It wouldn't take long for him to find out J.J.'s destination and follow her."

"But why? And why would Barb go along with it?"

"I think they are following the money," Slade let that sink in.

"J.J. knows what Ron did with the money!" Catherine was starting to see the events unfolding.

"She may have even helped him. Some of it went overseas and then disappeared. From what Fran and Helen have discovered some of the money disappeared from Canada, showed up again in the Caymans and then just disappeared. Ron and J.J. could have physically taken the money from there and hopped a small plane or chartered a jet anywhere and stashed it in safety deposit boxes. If J.J. has access, that is where she is going, to retrieve the money and disappear."

"Alright, I can understand why Petrov is after her, but why is Barb?"

"This morning I learned that Craig and Sam have determined that Ron used twenty million dollars of the firm's clients to fund the Syrian Way. If Barb has figured that out, she knows she must get that money back to her clients or lose the firm altogether. And she has very limited time to do it. In two months, the tax receipts won't be going out to her clients and everything will be out in the open."

"Oh, my God, she will be ruined! The firm is her legacy from her father. She will never be able to work in finance again. She must be desperate! Why didn't she come to me?"

"What could you do, Catherine, without the money? She knows this is the only way to get it back. My biggest concern is her being with Petrov. What kind of a deal has he made with her? And will he honor it? There is a lot we don't know about him, who he really is and what his agenda is."

Catherine nodded to him. "The CIA and Homeland Security are still not cooperating with us. Director Blanchette is trying diplomatic channels to force them, but I don't think he will succeed. They will use Homeland Security to hide behind." She rubbed her forehead.

"Try to get some rest, Catherine. The task force is continuing to dig for more information and we will know when they find anything." Slade knew Catherine was worried about her friend and he also knew she couldn't protect her if she was involved with Petrov or had anything to do with Ron's death. They were getting closer to those answers every mile they flew.

Chapter 30

The young handsome pilot helped J.J. down the stairs of the plane. With her big blue eyes, hour glass figure, and pouty lips she had him agreeing to her every whim. Petrov had put him on call at the airport waiting to see if Barb would try to escape or go after the money. This was when he thought she was involved as Ron had sworn she was. When J.J. booked the private jet this morning, Petrov was surprised. He was on his way to her office when he saw her leave and he was even more surprised to see Barb following her. Now, he thought, they are both going for the money.

The flight was long and tiring and J.J. knew she had burned her bridges behind her. She couldn't go back, she could only go forward with the plan she and Ron had made, their escape plan.

"You wait here for me. I will only be an hour or so and then we go on to San Paulo. "

"Yes, Miss. I'll be here," he kissed her fingers and smiled as he dropped the tracker in her big open purse. This was certainly one of his best assignments and he was feeling lucky today. Maybe he could spend some quality time with the sexy lady.

She had ordered a car with a driver from the plane and was soon on her way to the bank. She didn't realize she had company. The two-man team Catherine had put on her were following closely. She never even looked around. She was so focused on getting the money and she thought she was safe now. No one knew she was here.

Petrov's plane and the CSIS plane landed within ten minutes of each other. The CSIS plane landed first just as Catherine had thought, because it was the bigger jet. She was in contact with her men following J.J. and they were soon caught up with them at the bank. Petrov and Barb were right behind them following the tracker the pilot had apparently had succeeded in attaching to her.

Catherine by Evonne D. Haley

J.J. didn't realize she had so many eyes on her when she came out of the bank. She didn't care. She was in shock. The money was gone, the bearer bonds were gone, the diamonds were gone, the deposit box empty except for the note that read, 'Sorry, J.J.' in Ron's handwriting.

As she stumbled down the steps of the bank, Petrov and Barb each took one of her arms to lead her to their limo.

"Back to the airport," commanded Petrov to the driver as they got in the vehicle.

"It's gone, all gone," stammered J.J.

"What do you mean?" demanded Petrov.

"It's all gone. Ron took it somewhere and I don't know where. See," she passed him the note.

"Did he ever mention another bank or one in another country, a storage locker, anything?" Barb asked white faced.

"No, I can't believe he did this. I thought he loved me." J.J. started to cry, big sobs erupting from deep in her soul.

Barb looked at Petrov. "What now?"

"I need to think," he said distractedly.

No one spoke all the way back to the plane; just J. J's sob broke the silence. When they pulled up to the plane, Slade and Catherine were right behind them. Slade opened Petrov's door.

"Well, Detective. You have made a useless journey as well. The money is gone." Petrov was angry. Ron had out manoeuvred them all. He must be laughing in his grave. No wonder he had such a look of smug satisfaction on his face when Sameer killed him. Where would he have put the fortune he had stolen? At the moment, nobody knew; but Petrov was not known for giving up; he was known for his tenacity and his bulldog attitude. He wasn't calling it quits yet. He looked over at Barb and saw devastation on her beautiful face; that wasn't faked. Ron had kicked her even from the grave and she knew it. There was nothing left to do but to go home.

Petrov turned to Barb.

"Do you want to come back with me?" he asked her softly.

"No, I think she should return with us," said Catherine as she took Barb's hand. They would want to debrief her on the plane. She had a lot of questions she needed answers to.

"I will go with Catherine," Barb answered Petrov's question. "I will see you later?"

The question surprised everyone, including Barb herself.

"Yes, definitely." Petrov said looking into her eyes. He had every intention of seeing a lot of Barb in the future. "I will call you tomorrow." Petrov nodded his head to Catherine and Slade as he strode to his jet. They had no grounds to arrest him and couldn't outside Canada as they had no jurisdiction.

Catherine looked at Slade as they boarded the CSIS plane. Yes, they had a lot of questions for Barb as well as J.J.

After the debriefing Catherine and Slade knew no more than before. Barb had followed J.J. after hearing her conversation in the lunch room and had put two and two together and realized J.J. had been Ron's girlfriend. She told Catherine things had happened so quickly she didn't have time to call her and she had gone with Petrov, because she didn't want to lose J.J. Barb beseeched Catherine to remember that her entire career and the firm her father had left her was in peril because of Ron, and she had to get the money back or lose everything.

J.J.'s debriefing had brought some new details to light. Especially, the trips to Costa Rica and Ron's betrayal of his girlfriend. There was no hint of where Ron had hidden the money from there. Converting some of the money into diamonds and bearer bonds had been brilliant as there were so many places he could have hidden them. He could have put them into another safety deposit box in any bank in the world or he could have buried them in the back yard. They would question J.J.

extensively over the next few days, but there was nothing they could do to her, no charges to lay. She had just gone on vacation with her boyfriend. They were at a dead end.

Chapter 31

Barb and her girls were decorating their Christmas tree a week later when Catherine, Maggie and Ella and their children arrived to help them celebrate the season of Christ's birth. Even Maggie's son was there. Only Ella's son, Andrew, was missing. He was on a dig in South America and couldn't make it home for Christmas. The rest of the group were all so happy to see each other; there was a very festive spirit surrounding them all as they finished decorating the tree. The ladies had brought appetizers and presents.

When Barb went to the kitchen to get more wine glasses, Catherine followed her. Barb seemed to be very happy for a change.

"How are things with you, Barb?" she asked.

"Great! I was going to call you but got too busy. I received a call from Dad's lawyer yesterday. You will never guess what Dad had done. He took out a twenty-million-dollar life insurance policy on Ron! Can you believe that!

Now, I can replace the money Ron stole from my clients. I will still have to placate them, but with the insurance money I think most will stay with my company. I am so relieved and happy! I was sure I had lost everything. I didn't tell the girls as I didn't want to ruin their Christmas and stress them out over exams. They knew I was worried but now I can be happy and that makes them happy. They are going back on Sunday to write their exams and finish out the year. It will be great for them to get back to a normal life now that Sameer is dead."

Catherine hugged her. She was surprised Barb hadn't called her yesterday with the great news, but then she knew how busy everyone was this time of year and she knew she would be seeing her today. Whatever, it was all working out for Barb and she was happy for her. Slade was taking her out to dinner tomorrow night and she would tell him of Barb's great news then. He would be happy for her, too.

"Come in here, you two." Called Maggie. "We are waiting to open the presents."

■■■

The next evening Catherine was telling Slade about Barb's serendipitous luck. He looked at her when she finished.

"What is it? You don't seem as relieved as I thought you would be." He reached for her hand.

"I don't know. Maybe it is just that Ron had negatively affected Barb's life for so long, it is hard for me to believe he can't hurt her anymore."

"Or?"

"It just seems to too good to be true. Barb's father was a good man. He could have done that for her knowing Ron would someday get himself killed, as he was so dishonest and a bully, that someone would come after him eventually." Catherine was frowning.

241

Catherine by Evonne D. Haley

"And I say again, or?" Slade grinned at her.

"Persistent aren't you," she smiled back at him. He was learning more about her all the time.

"Well, why would she lie to me and where would she get the money?"

"I think the first thing is to determine if she really received the insurance money. You can go from there."

"But Slade, I feel so disloyal to even think she would lie to me." She gripped his hand.

"But, you do, don't you?"

"Yes, I'm afraid I do." She admitted.

Slade pulled into the valet parking and then escorted Catherine into the restaurant. They had a wonderful meal and their conversation stayed light as they talked about their childhoods, life events, favourite movies and future goals.

"Will you come to my parent's home for Christmas dinner with me, Cat?" Slade asked holding her hand as they waited for the valet to get his car.

"Yes, I would love to, Jeremy. What better way to get to know someone than to talk to his parents and family. I am sure they have lots of stories to tell me." She laughed at his expression of horror.

"Ah, maybe I should take back that invitation." He was half serious as he thought of all the stories she would hear, especially from his brother. "That's not fair. I can't reciprocate."

Catherine had no one to rat her out. She had no family left to tell tales about her. Her family now was Maggie and Ella and their families. She smiled an elfish grin at him. They could give him an earful, but she wouldn't tell him that.

As he pulled up in front of her apartment building, she said, "Do you want to come up for a coffee? It's still quite early."

Slade studied her. She was nervous, twisting her hands on her purse strap and when she finally looked up at him, she was blushing.

"I would love to. Maybe we could watch a movie? Or fool around?" He waggled his eyebrows in a pretend leer.

Catherine had to laugh at his way of lightening what could have been an awkward moment. She gave him instructions to go back around the building to the underground parking.

When the elevator stopped on her floor she became nervous again. She knew Slade would never force the physical issue of their relationship, but she also knew how strong her feelings were for him. Maybe she didn't trust herself around him.

Slade helped her remove her coat and she took his to hang in the closet.

"Go sit and relax, Jeremy. I will make us some coffee."

Instead of turning to go to the living room, he stepped into her personal space and took her into his arms while staring into her eyes. She fit perfectly. With heels her head came to just below the bottom of his chin. He smiled, perfectly relaxed. Catherine smiled back, relaxing into his hold. His eyes moved to her mouth as he leaned in to kiss her.

Yes, she thought. This man was beginning to hold her heart. His lips were gentle at first; and then, as if he couldn't help himself, his embrace became stronger and his lips were more demanding, passionate, taking her breath away. This could escalate into so much more. Gradually, Slade gentled the embrace and leaned back a little. His gaze on her face was not quite smiling, more of a grimace.

"I don't know if this was a good idea, Catherine, us being unchaperoned." His gaze was serious.

"Well, we could put the pillows between us on the couch to watch a movie." She smiled trying to tease him into a lighter mood.

He smiled back. He loved her sense of humor and knew she realized how easily this could turn into a passionate affair.

Ok. I've got myself under control. We shouldn't need a barrier between us to watch a movie." Suddenly he became serious. "I have to tell you, Catherine. My desire for you is not just sexual. I really care for you and from your responses to me, I think you care for me as well. I am a straight shooter. We could do this dance around each other for months, but I don't want to. I want to build a relationship with you. I have never felt like this before and I need to know how you feel about me. Are we on the same path?" Slade was nervous putting it all on the line like this. He thought he knew her well enough to know she wasn't one to play games with him and his heart.

"Slade, I care for you and I'm anxious to see where this is going, too. To be honest I never thought I would be in this situation. I am addicted to my work. I was married for two years and when I found out I was pregnant, he left. He didn't want children. I did, but my baby was stillborn. I never wanted to go through that again or even attempt it, so I focused totally on my career. But then I met you." She leaned in and gave him a quick kiss and wrapped her arms around his waist.

"Maybe I was waiting for you. Yes, I think we are on the same path, so let's relax and enjoy the journey. Ok?"

"Ok, Catherine." He grinned down at her knowing she was his. He hugged her tight as she laid her face against his chest. She fit so perfectly.

"Let's snuggle on the couch and watch a movie." He let her go and headed to the kitchen to make the popcorn.

■■■

On Saturday Maggie was in Catherine and Barb's building showing a condo for sale when she saw Peter Petrov leaving the building. What was he doing here? When her clients had left, she went up to Barb's on a hunch. Barb answered her knock.

"Did you forget something, Peter?" The words were out of her mouth before she had opened the door all the way.

"Oh, Maggie, it's you. Come in. Would you like a coffee?"

Maggie stepped into the foyer. "Sure, that would be great. I was showing a condo in the building, so I thought I would see if you were in."

Barb took her coat.

"I'm just puttering around, doing weekend chores. Come in to the kitchen." She laid Maggie's coat over a barstool at the counter.

"Your place is spotless as usual. I don't know how you do it, working full time. I'm such a pig, my place always seems messy."

She took a mug of coffee from Barb as she sat at the counter.

"You work even on weekends, Maggie. You don't have time to clean. Besides I have a part time housekeeper, who comes in one afternoon a week and she is really great. Actually, she is looking for a few new clients. I think you would like her and it would take housekeeping off your plate."

"You know, I have been thinking of doing that. I just felt that I should be able to handle it, but I am working all the time. And you're right. It would take a lot of stress off me."

Barb wrote a name and number on the to-do-list pad on her fridge and gave Maggie the slip of paper.

"Here you are, Maggie. She does the floors, bathrooms, kitchen and dusts throughout. She is fast and efficient. Let me know how you make out with her."

"Thanks, Barb, for this and the coffee. I won't take up any more of your Saturday." Maggie headed for the door as she put on her coat.

"It was nice to see you, Maggie. We must get together with the girls soon." Barb smiled.

She seemed happier than Maggie had seen her in a while.

"I can set that up. How about two weeks from next Saturday? We could all go out for dinner, just us four ladies after all the holiday celebrations are over?" At Barb's nod, she said, "See you next weekend, hopefully, for Christmas. I will get back to you tomorrow after I check with everyone." Maggie turned and gave a small wave as she headed for the elevator. She needed to talk to Catherine.

Chapter 32

Petrov headed to the warehouse. He had several activities to complete, but his mind was on Barb Delong, as it was all the time now. She fascinated him. She was not only beautiful, she was smart, independent. She could also be lying, to everyone, not just him, but to her friends as well. He had gotten to know her some during their six-hour flight to Costa Rica. Since they returned, he had called her several times and even visited her twice. She was gracious and forthcoming with her news that saved her business and reputation.

There was just something not quite right, more a feeling he couldn't get rid of. That is why he bugged her condo during his visit today. He had placed a small device under her counter as he sat on the stool in her kitchen. On top of that was his attraction to her; and unless he was reading her signals wrong, it was reciprocated. He would see what results he got from the surveillance and go from there.

■■■

If nothing else, Petrov was a determined man. Rarely was he blown off course. He was often relentless until he obtained what he wanted. And he wanted Barb Delong; he also wanted the money that Ron had stolen. He planned to get both.

··

Catherine was in her office going over photos of the terrorist van. The five men in the van had been positively identified from surveillance videos as the men in Sameer's cell. The fingerprints of the dead man on the docks that they thought was Sameer were not a positive match to anyone in the CSIS database or any other branch of security in Canada or the United States, including Homeland Security and even Interpol. They were going on just pictures and his features were not identifiable due to the gunshot exit wound, but his build and height were similar, and he was wearing the same jacket he had on in some of the other surveillance photos they had taken of him previously.

Catherine and the others had assumed it was Sameer; but now that they couldn't 100% positively identify him, Catherine felt fear clinch her chest. What if he was still out there? Then the twins were not safe and she had taken their security detail off them. She would fix that with a phone call. Barb, too, needed to be watched. At this point all three would be bait, but with guards doubled and 24/7 surveillance. She didn't like it, but it was what it was, whether she like it or not. Without a positive ID on Sameer or his dead double, Catherine knew he was out there plotting a new terrorist act and he needed money for that, Delong's money that he thought Barb had. Things hadn't changed at all.

Catherine's phone rang,

"Hello, Catherine Henley speaking."

"Hi, it's me, Maggie." She paused. "I have something to tell you. I don't want to get anyone in trouble, but I think this is something you should know."

"Ok, Maggie. Go ahead. I won't shoot the messenger."

"I just left Barb. I think she is seeing Peter Petrov. I saw him in her building while I was showing a condo here. So, I stopped in to see her, and when she opened the door, she said, "Did you forget something, Peter?""

There was silence as Catherine tried to compute this information.

"Well, thanks Maggie. You were right. This is something I should know. I will take it from here. Please keep this confidential. It may not have been Petrov she was talking about, but I will look into it."

"I won't say anything, Catherine. I'm sorry." Maggie hated dealing with awkward situations, but she would rather face them head on than let them fester into something worse.

Catherine by Evonne D. Haley

"You don't need to be sorry, honey. I'm glad you called me. I will see you Wednesday for lunch."

"Ok. See you then." A subdued Maggie hung up.

Catherine sat looking at her desk for a minute and then she picked up her phone.

"Slade. I need to see you in my office if you have a minute. Great. See you in five."

Slade was like her, working on a Saturday. Everyone on the task force was in the conference room working on the case. She had gone to her office for some quiet time to think. Every time she thought she had found a lead, something else popped up to confound her thinking. Petrov and Barb? This was a whole new game, especially if Sameer wasn't dead.

Slade knocked as he walked in. "What do you have?"

Catherine filled him in on Barb and Petrov and then she hit him with the news that

Sameer might still be out there getting ready to hit Toronto or another large city.

"The fact that worries me the most is where will he get the money? Will he go after Barb? If he even thinks she has it, he won't hesitate to take her or her girls. He is probably waiting for more men to get here before he acts, as his cell was wiped out." She paused then looked up at Slade. "What if he killed his own men and a dummy so we would think it was him? That would give him some wiggle room to stay in Toronto and get another cell working. Barb and her girls won't be safe and it won't be easy on them to go through all of this again."

Catherine stopped to take a breath. As she looked up at Slade, he spoke.

"If she has found the money, would she keep it all? If her father didn't take out an insurance policy on Ron, that means she must have found the money. And that means she lied to you. But the biggest question is does Petrov know? Are they in on it together?

Those are very important unanswered questions."

Slade watched Catherine as she mulled it all over in her head. It was painful for him to see her working the scenarios in her head, especially when they all led to the conclusion that Barb had not only lied to her, but that she could have committed an illegal act.

"Can you find out if she received the insurance money?"

"We still have access to her financial records through the subpoena, so if she put money from the insurance into the company accounts, we can see it and backtrack to her personal accounts. Also, every cash transaction over ten thousand must be reported through the bank. I just hate to have to do this, but I will put Fran or Helen on it."

Slade knew how this must be weighing on her, to suspect her friend.

"Still no ID on the murder victim on the docks? That could mean he was here illegally as part of Sameer's cell. There are still two finger prints not matched to anyone in the van. Does that mean one could be Sameer's?

"Most likely. We don't have his on file and they don't match the body on the docks. We are working on getting Petrov's DNA. I don't want to use Barb, but if he is visiting her, we could get it from a coffee cup, wine glass, etc. That would cross off one part of this case, if it proves he is Delong's brother. But it also creates another question. Is there a Russian influence in this terrorist activity? That is a more important question to answer. We also need to question why Delong changed his name and his looks, if he is Petrov's brother. What would be his reasoning for doing it? Did the fact he worked in finance be part of a bigger plot to gain money for a hit on Canadian or US soil? We know these cells can work for years to strike at their enemy. They will want revenge for Ron stealing the missing funds."

"My God! Barb could be in even more danger than before. Sameer will not just need the money. He will want revenge for the shame of failing to complete the job."

Catherine by Evonne D. Haley

"Catherine, let's put surveillance on the twins and Barb, 24/7, three teams on each so we don't get caught with our pants down like before. If Sameer is going to try to hit the city, will it be the same target as before? Do we have any intel on that?"

"Yes, we had some chatter on the Tower or possibly the Arena. Both are well known landmarks with a lot of collateral damage, as well as the significance such an attack would make. Let's go meet with the task force team to see what new information we have."

Slade held the door open for her. "Are you prepared to talk about the new information on Barb?"

"Yes, I think so. If she is innocent, that will show and if she's in league with Petrov to go after the money, that will show as well. Either way the most important goal to keep in mind is the possible attack. There are many people in jeopardy, not just Barb. The truth will come out. I just want us to find it before anyone gets hurt."

As they entered the conference room, they saw the room was buzzing. Something was happening.

"What's going on, Roger?" Slade's chief of staff was co-ordinating with Marianne and Ren, who were trying to put together all the information that was coming in faster that they could compile it.

"Sam and Craig broke through the last firewall on Delong's computer. He really knew what he was doing when he coded the information. Our boys are great, but together they are unbelievable. They should work as a team all the time. Seriously, boss. Think about that. Anyway, Fran and Helen found a string and pulled it on the financial quagmire he had created. It must have taken years for him to develop this many layered shell companies. Ren found the connection between the money path and those shell companies."

"Yes," said Marianne. "Ren and I have enough to give a quick report. We will dig further, but I think this is plenty to go on."

Slade and Catherine took their seats. "Ok, let's see what we have so far." Slade waved at the screen that came down from the ceiling.

"To begin with, Delong was brilliant in many ways and a total moron in others. According to the records found in the protected files on his computer, he has been developing layers of shell companies for three years. He had a labyrinth of companies with hundreds of shell companies, but now we know the names we can find the trail back to Sameer. Ron was either going to use them to embezzle money from Barb's firm and disappear, which would have been my guess, or he was going to fund a small war. According to his files, and this is where he was a moron, he accounted for every dollar that he took from his firm's clients and from the online NPO businesses that he had funneled money through.

From the online sites he raked in over eighty million dollars; from his firm he stole over twenty million and laundered it through the NPOs and the shell companies for a total of over one hundred million. He may have had more NPOs and websites, but it will take us longer to find that out. We will start by going through all the shell companies to see if money was deposited from more websites. However, we still don't know where he hid the money, but I would guess it was somewhere other than bank accounts, probably in diamonds, gold or even real estate in or out of this country.

Delong seemed to be obsessed with documenting every dollar so somewhere he must have documented what he did with the money. We still have a lot to go through, so I am sure we will find it. It could be as simple as a receipt for a safe; let's hope so anyway."

"Roger, did you find out if Petrov bought those expensive leather Gucci shoes?" asked Slade. "With the exclusive symbol on the soles?"

"Yes, he did, but that doesn't prove they were his at the crime scene. We will have to get a subpoena to search his condo to get his shoes and test for Delong's blood on them."

"Yes, and it would be one more fact that will ultimately help convict him." Catherine said. "Also, Roger, would you please assign three teams of 24/7 surveillance on Barb Delong, and her girls. Sameer may not be dead; and if he isn't, it will just be a matter of time before he goes after them.

The teams are to be very alert at all times. We don't want another disaster and lose more agents. Plus, I think we need to look at the Russian angle to see if it is just coincidence or if there is a Russian factor in Sameer's cell and this terrorist threat.

Ren, could you take that on? Go back through all the old information and what is now coming in. See if there is any Russian company, bank, name or grandmother.

You guys are great and I must say Roger is correct. You work extremely well as a team. Keep it up and we will close this case. Then you can all take a two-week vacation. You've certainly put in the overtime for it."

"Thanks, Catherine. We will have a full report by tomorrow morning, say nine o'clock?" Roger was looking at his team and they all nodded. The sooner they finished this job, the sooner those vacation days could start.

Slade stood up. "Friday is Christmas Eve. It would be nice to have this finished by then; but even if we don't, let's all take the weekend off, unless something drastic happens we can spend the holiday with our families. The break will be good and could help us refocus when we get back. If, however, there is any chatter or intelligence that reveals an attack over the holidays, we will all have to be here. There could be a lot of lives at stake."

Everyone was nodding. They knew what the outcome could be and they would all do what was needed to be done to save lives. This was their job. It was what they had signed up for.

Slade's cell phone was vibrating in his pocket. He took it out and noted the number.

"Sorry, I have to take this." He stepped out into the hall. "Hello, Chuck. Good to hear from you. Are you in town?"

"Hi, Slade. Could we meet up?" Chuck's voice was serious.

"Sure. Where and when?" Slade knew this was business. His brother worked for a military section of the government.

"I am down the street." That was their code for a diner where they often met.

"Give me a few minutes. Is it OK if I bring someone with me?" Slade asked.

There was a pause. "Someone from work?"

"Yes." Slade responded. Now he knew it was serious business.

"OK. See you in ten." Chuck hung up. He knew Jeremy would only bring someone in their line of work who could be trusted implicitly. Chuck's job was not advertised to the public. Even his parents didn't know exactly what he did.

Catherine by Evonne D. Haley

Slade opened the door to the conference room and motioned for Catherine to come out into the hall. When she got to him, he leaned into the room and said to the task force team, "We will be back in an hour."

"And where will we be coming back from?" Catherine asked as he ushered her into the elevator to the parking garage.

"I want you to meet someone," was the cryptic reply.

"Ok, will I need my coat?"

"No, I will loan you mine."

"OK then."

Ten minutes later they entered the diner. Chuck was sitting in the farthest booth in the back. He and Slade did the hug and backslapping routine, while smiling at each other. "Really great to see you, brother. It's been far too long."

Chuck agreed and then turned to Catherine. "I know we've never met before, because I would remember you." He smiled at her as he took her hand.

"Down, Chuck. Get your own girl. This one's mine." Said Slade.

"Really? Well, that's good for you and bad for me."

Catherine looked at both men and smiled. They were very alike in looks and manner. She liked Chuck, but she could also see his smile wasn't quite reflected in his eyes. They were sober.

They settled themselves in the booth and gave their orders to the waitress.

"Catherine is with CSIS." Slade told his brother softly.

Chuck nodded.

"And you, Chuck. Who are you with?" asked Catherine.

"I am with military intelligence. I wanted to give you a heads up before I join your task force tomorrow. We have some information you may already know. We have heard through the grapevine that there is a level four threat on the Tower. Our sources say it is set for the 23rd, the day before Christmas Eve. There will be a lot of people there and the restaurant at the top is fully booked for the evening with a few big names attending. The strike will be more of a religious statement due to the fact that it is one day before Christmas Eve than the amount of people they can kill. Even though Christmas is not observed as religious holiday now by many Canadians, it is still a nationally observed holiday held sacred by Christians."

"Yes, we heard the chatter, although we didn't know if it was the Tower or the Sports Center. Are you sure of your intel? They could kill more people at the Center, thousands more."

"No, our intel is good. Our source is one hundred percent positive and we are ninety-nine percent positive of our source. The one percent is my pessimistic side of the possibility of someone becoming a traitor. Personally, I believe it is one hundred percent positive."

"It's you, isn't it?" frowned Slade.

"Do you have any suspects that you know are here in the City?" Chuck avoided Slade's question with one for Catherine.

"We do. He goes by the name of Sameer." Catherine went on to explain the case so far.

"We have heard that name as being the leader; but if he lost his cell, we would assume he would have to go back home to get more recruits or go underground until he had more money to hire mercenaries here. Either way that will take time, which doesn't go with the plan on December 23rd." Chuck's thoughts were troubled as he knew from his sources that the plan was still on.

"What about the Russian, Petrov? How deep do you think he is with Sameer? Is he more than just an arm's dealer? We didn't have any reports on him to suspect otherwise. From what you're telling me he has a big stake in this, and if Sameer killed his brother, if Delong was his brother, what is Petrov's plan now?"

"There are too many 'ifs' in this scenario. We need to firm up some of these answers." Slade continued.

"Alright, I am going to see what I can find out about Petrov at my end. I will call you later, Jeremy. Nice to meet you, Catherine. Will you be at Mom and Dad's for Christmas dinner?" He grinned knowing Jeremy had not brought a girl home for Christmas in years. This was putting his brother on the spot and Chuck wanted to see what Jeremy would do to squirm out of it.

To his surprise, Catherine smiled right back at him. "I will be there if this all doesn't blow up in our faces."

Chuck almost choked. This was more serious than he had thought. He looked at Jeremy; he was grinning from ear to ear.

. . . .

Petrov was finishing up the details of the hit on the Tower. His team was ready and eager for the final act. They had been training for three months. Sameer had presumed he was in charge, but he never was. Petrov had been calling the shots from day one. Sameer had been cowed by Petrov, because he was a much more domineering personality and he had some very highly placed connections in Russia.

When Sameer found out Delong was Petrov's brother after he killed him, he knew his time was limited. He also knew Petrov was as dedicated to this mission as he was due to his own agenda, so he would put up with Sameer until it was done. Sameer planned to be on his way back home before Petrov could get to him, but his main goal was for the attack to be successful. If that meant dying to finish it, he would. That was the difference between them. Sameer didn't think Petrov would give his life for the cause; and that made Sameer more powerful, because he had nothing to lose. Petrov did.

Chapter 33

Monday morning Catherine called Maggie to tell her she had to cancel lunch on Wednesday.

"This is a work-related issue, isn't it? Ok, I know you can't talk about it. Will we see you Christmas Eve?" Maggie knew it was a serious matter for Catherine to cancel.

"I really hope so, but at this point, I cannot guarantee it. I will call you before then to let you know." Catherine was trying to reassure Maggie and probably herself as well. "Would you call Ella for me?"

"Sure, Catherine. You keep safe, OK?"

"That's the plan, Maggie. We will talk again later in the week." Catherine was hanging up when Director Blanchette and Chuck Slade came into her office.

"Good morning, Sir, Chuck." She greeted him with a smile.

"Good morning, Catherine. I hear you met Chuck Slade yesterday. Hopefully, with his team from military intelligence and our task

272

force, we can get this wrapped up by this weekend. Chuck here has a stellar reputation, a good man."

Chuck must be high in military intelligence to get Blanchette on board so easily. Things are going to happen fast now, thought Catherine.

"I will let you take him to meet the task force and we will be coordinating all our efforts to take down this group of terrorists. Keep me apprised." He nodded his head at her as he left.

"Hi, Chuck."

"Good morning, Catherine. I left four of my men at the elevators and we are ready to get to work. We have new intel on the Tower attack and only a few hours to coordinate our efforts to take them down."

"Finally, we may have a break then. Let's go get everyone brought up to speed. Follow me, please." Catherine turned to lead the way.

As Chuck followed Catherine down the hall he couldn't help but think that his brother, Jeremy, was a very lucky man.

They picked up Chuck's men at the elevators and went to the conference room where all the team was hard at work.

Jeremy looked up and smiled when he saw Catherine enter with Chuck and his team.

"Everyone, this is Chuck Slade and his team from Military Intelligence. They have intel on Sameer's cell and the planned attack. Chuck, please introduce your men and bring us up to date." Catherine went to her seat by Jeremy and let Chuck take over the meeting.

As he started to introduce his men, his eyes swept over the white board with Petrov's picture on it.

"I see you have Peter Petrov's picture on the board?" he asked.

"We believe Petrov is involved with Sameer and may be selling arms to him. Why?" asked Catherine.

"Remember when I said I would find out more about Petrov? He is not an arms dealer; well, not really. He could be acting the part of one. He is an asset of the CIA."

Catherine and Slade looked at each other. Now they knew why the two feds in Blanchette's office acted so strange.

"Well, that puts a different spin on it. What is his role in all of this?"

"We are not exactly sure. We have heard that he is playing Sameer, but for what reason, nobody knows. It could be that he is trying to find a Russian influence with Sameer's cell. There has been chatter that the Russians are financing ISIS, so Petrov could be going after the man who is now supplying funds to Sameer, especially after he lost the money Delong stole."

"Do you have surveillance on Petrov?" Chuck asked.

"24/7." Replied Catherine.

Chapter 34

Petrov sat at his desk thinking about Barb Delong. He was sure she found the money and there was a rumor on the street that a deal had been made for the sale of over thirty million in diamonds; more than enough to bail her out of the mess Delong had left her in. But this begged the questions; did she just sell what she needed to save her firm, did she have the rest of the money in diamonds; and if so, where were they?

He was taking her out for dinner at seven this evening. He was hoping she would confess that she had the money. They had been seeing each other since the flight to Costa Rica. He had to admit that he was very attracted to her, but he knew he would protect her with everything he had, because she had been Alexi's wife. She was family. He wanted to have her as his wife, but there were a lot of obstacles in his way; the biggest being Barb herself. He felt she was attracted to him and he had been using that attraction to bring her closer to him.

He had three major events he needed to happen. The first was to finish the job he was being paid to complete; the second was to kill Sameer for killing his brother; and the last, but most important, was to get out of the country, if it all went haywire, and take Barb and the girls with him.

He already had the last event in play. There was tight security around Barb and her girls, but his men were prepared for that. They were patient and diligent. It would just take a slip in security, a bathroom break, a distraction. Petrov was expecting word at any time that the girls were in his care. He would take Barb at dinner tonight. He had reserved a table at the Tower and had his men prepared to take her out the back through the kitchen into the van and be gone before her security could act. He would act like the concerned date, getting angry, pushing the police to find her.

The first item on his list would be finished on Thursday with the second item completed along with the terrorist act. Sameer would be killed and blamed for the bombing as well, vengeance satisfied. The attack was a subterfuge for the assignation of the Russian Ambassador, who was the link to ISIS providing arms and intelligence information to terrorist cells in the US and Canada. No one would link the assassination and the bombing. Sameer didn't know he was the goat tied to the post. He thought he was the leader when, in fact, he was the fall guy. He would take all the blame and Petrov would win it all, the money for killing the traitor, plus his vengeance satisfied by killing his brother's murderer; and he would have Barb, his nieces and the money left from his brother's illegal acts. He knew Barb had the money. He didn't know how or when she acquired it, but she had it.

■■

Because of Petrov and his infatuation with Delong's wife and her kids, he had brought too much attention on Sameer. To throw off the authorities, Sameer had killed the man on the docks by shooting him in the back of the head with a large caliber gun to destroy his face and dental attributes so the authorities wouldn't be able to identify him as not being Sameer. He also had killed his five men in the van to protect himself and his backup cell of five unidentified men. The five men he had killed had died for the cause and their deaths would be talked about for years in their homeland. They would be heroes. Sameer had to kill them because the authorities were too close, and because the twins could identify them. All this trouble he blamed on Petrov. And now he had to make sure Petrov didn't interfere with his plans and destroy the mission. To do that Sameer put a man on Petrov to keep him informed of his actions. If he had to, Sameer would kill Petrov. Nothing would interfere with the attack on Thursday.

Chapter 35

Petrov picked Barb up at her condo at seven-thirty that evening. They had reservations at one of the best restaurants in the city, the revolving restaurant at the top of the Tower. He had reserved a window table with a spectacular view. As the room turned you got a three-hundred-sixty-degree view of the City; but it wasn't the view that Petrov was there for. It wasn't even just to impress Barb. It was also reconnaissance; even though he had been there several times before, he wanted to see the layout and where the Ambassador would be sitting. He had put one of his men inside as a new waiter and he was a very good waiter. He knew how to talk to people and put them at ease. Tonight, he was serving them. Barb was smiling and talking to him as he lightly flirted with her. Petrov was frowning at him as he left to get their drink orders. Barb smiled slightly as she looked at Petrov.

"Are you jealous of a waiter, Peter?"

280

Catherine by Evonne D. Haley

He looked into her eyes.

"Yes."

Barb's smile wavered. Ron used to be jealous of waiters, valets and even a man who held the door open for her once. She wasn't going through that again.

Petrov took her hand. He had sat beside her instead of across from her for just this reason. He knew how awkward it could be reaching across the table, plus she could retreat from him more easily. Just as she was trying to do now. He gently kept her from pulling her hand away.

"Yes," he reiterated, "I am jealous of the smiles you give to other men. I want you to smile at me, to flirt with me, to be mine, my lover, and, soon, my wife. I can be patient to get what I want, Barbara, but I want you to know this. You are my future. I will keep you safe, and I will keep your girls safe, as I did before."

"What do you mean? You will keep them safe, as you did before? You tried to take them to Russia, away from me." Her voice was rising with every word.

He tightened his grip on her hand.

"Yes, but I kept them safe as I am doing now." He said softly.

Her eyes widened.

"You have my girls, Peter?" she whispered.

"Yes, they are safe. No one will hurt them."

Barb looked him in the eyes.

"What do you want?" Her gaze was now cold as ice. This was a mother who would do anything to protect her children.

"I want you to trust me. There are some events planned and I want to be sure you and the twins will be safe, protected. I can't do that if I don't know where you are."

Barb was thinking this through.

"How long?"

"Just for a few days."

"And then?" she pushed him for answers.

282

"Then, that is up to you." Peter stroked her hand with his thumb.

"I would like to go home now and I want to talk to my girls."

"Yes, you can talk to the girls from the car, but going home is not an option right now. Now, stand up and go with our waiter like he is showing you to the washroom."

Petrov motioned to the waiter. When he quickly came to their table, Barb stood up to go with him. Petrov stood also, leaned into her and softly said, "I also want the seventy million you have left in diamonds."

Barb closed her eyes. Petrov didn't know it, but he had just made it near impossible to get to the rest of the diamonds.

Chapter 36

Catherine, Slade and Chuck along with the rest of the team were all in the conference room when the call came in that Barb had disappeared from the restaurant where she had gone to dinner with Petrov. Apparently, he was furious that they weren't doing enough to find her.

"Chuck, do you want to come with us or stay here?"

"I will stay here and get caught up with the team, thanks." Chuck's attention was focused on all the information that the team had already gathered.

"Ok, see you in a bit," replied Slade.

Slade and Catherine left immediately, but continued to talk to the team leader at the crime scene on Slade's cell. The waiter who had shown Barb to the washroom had also disappeared. The assumption was that he took her. There were cameras all around the

Tower, but none showed her leaving with him. The restaurant was now closed off as a crime scene and all the patrons and staff were being questioned as to what they had seen, thought, or heard. It could be quite enlightening when pulling thoughts from witnesses as it usually came from seeing or hearing something that they wouldn't have deemed important, but could be vital.

Slade and Catherine entered the restaurant after signing in to the crime scene recorder. The first thing they saw was a furious Petrov, who was threatening to call the Mayor, the Chief of Police and a bevy of other high-ranking city officials.

When he saw Slade and Catherine, he practically ran to them.

"Where is she? Do you know who took her? What are you doing to get her back? Is it Sameer? No, no he's dead. He couldn't have done it."

Petrov was gasping as he shot all the questions to them.

285

Catherine by Evonne D. Haley

"Let's sit down here for a moment, Peter." Said Slade as helped him into a chair. "Take a minute to catch your breath. Would you like some water?"

When he nodded, Slade looked at Catherine who rolled her eyes, but then left to get him some water. When she returned, Slade passed the bottle of water to Petrov. After he took a drink, Slade said calmly, "Now, walk us through this. Start when you left to pick Barb up." Slade wanted him to fill in some holes of the events for them and to verify what their surveillance team had reported at their end. Plus, he wanted to see how Petrov would play this out.

"I left at seven to pick her up. My driver drove directly to her condo. I got out of the car, when she came down the steps to the car and I gave her a kiss. We left there and drove directly to the restaurant. My driver opened the car door and we went into the Tower. The elevator took us to the restaurant at the top of the building. The manager, Tomas, seated us at our table by the window. We talked of our

286

future and I ordered champagne. As we waited for it, Barb asked where the washrooms were. When I waved the waiter over to ask, he offered to escort her there. She never came back. I called the police. That's it. Now what are you doing to find her?" His voice had risen toward the end of his speech and he was getting wound up again.

Slade had been taking notes and Catherine had turned her recorder on her phone when she went to get his water.

Slade looked up from his notes and then said, "Did the waiter come back?"

"The waiter? Who cares about the waiter!? I want to get Barb back!"

"We think the waiter took her out through the kitchen access for deliveries. Had you ever seen him before?"

"No, I don't think so," Petrov answered frowning.

"Do you have any enemies that would do this to get to you? Give us the first couple that come to mind." Catherine asked him derisively.

Petrov looked at her. Her anger at him was coming through in her tone and questions. "Yes, I do have some enemies, but the only one I can think of that would do this would be Sameer and he is dead."

Catherine shot Slade a look and then looked down, but Petrov caught it. So, he thought. They know Sameer isn't dead or they just cannot prove he isn't. That was good. He needed them to believe Sameer was still the leader of this coming threat.

When he first got involved with Sameer, it was strictly business, to sell him a few guns and ammunition, to see who he dealt with and to find out who funded him. When Ron got involved, it was for the money. Petrov wanted out; out of being under the thumb of the US government, to be free. He never intended to give the money to Sameer; some maybe, but not all. He and Ron were going to split the major portion. Then Sameer found out Ron had stolen the money and got angry. Before Petrov could stop him, Sameer shot Ron right in front of him. Even before Ron told them where the money was. For that alone Petrov vowed to kill Sameer. Getting him to take the fall for the attack was genius, not only for Sameer to be the scapegoat, but to cover the assassination of the Russian Ambassador.

Taking Barb here tonight was also part of his plan to get to the Ambassador. The restaurant would be closed as it was a crime scene, but the Mayor would see it reopened by Thursday, as he was part of the guest list for that evening of December 23rd. After closing the restaurant for two days, when they opened on the morning of the 23rd, there would be a stampede of deliveries, chefs, waiters, and other staff; a perfect cover for his man to plant the shaped charge, which would focus the effect of the explosive's energy toward the Ambassador.

His man was also to make sure the Ambassador sat in the seat with the best view of the city. This bomb and one other were remotely controlled; the assassination would be completed even if Sameer screwed things up. Petrov knew the timing would be tight and many things could go wrong, so Sameer would also play a role as Petrov's backup plan. Petrov knew he could just let Sameer do the job for him, but he wanted to make sure the job was completed and that the Ambassador didn't walk away. He knew Sameer would check the timer on his bomb ten minutes before it was to go off. He had control issues, serious control issues. So, Petrov would detonate his bomb early while Sameer was in the building, two birds with one stone, so to speak.

Right now, however, Petrov had to be convincing about his concern for Barb in front of Slade and Catherine.

"Sameer is dead, isn't he?" He asked, his face was masked with fear.

"We haven't positively identified the body as his yet." Catherine answered. "What is your connection to Sameer, Petrov? Did you two do business together? We've heard you sell arms and munitions to just about anyone. Have you sold him ammunition to make an assault on our city?"

"No, I haven't dealt with him in any capacity like that." Petrov stated seriously. "I was importing beautiful, priceless pieces of art from his homeland, Iran, that were owned by his family. He was afraid they would be confiscated by his government or destroyed."

Catherine was amazed at his audacity while admiring his plausibility. He seemed so genuinely concerned over Barb.

"Really? That's your story? That is what you want us to believe? How does Ron Delong fit in with this story?"

Petrov looked directly into Catherine's eyes and said, "Ron was my brother."

"Does Barb know that?" Catherine didn't even flinch.

"No, I haven't told her yet."

Catherine by Evonne D. Haley

"Explain you and Ron to me." Catherine asked him. She didn't believe anything he was telling her, but she wanted to hear his story.

"When we were young boys, our parents were killed at Chernobyl in 1986. They were physicists at the site. We were fostered out in different homes. When Alexi was twenty-one, he moved to New York City to finish his Masters Degree in Business. He changed his name for some strange reason, I don't know why, and we lost touch. I hadn't heard from him in years until I saw his picture in the Toronto newspaper and the story of his murder. I went to the funeral to meet his wife and to see if I could be of help to her. She seemed to take my greetings as an insult, when all I wanted was to keep her and her twin daughters from harm."

"What about the kidnapping of the twins? Were you just helping to keep them safe then?" Slade asked him.

"Yes," Petrov looked very serious.

"Did you know Sameer before that?"

292

"Yes," he said again. "Like I said, I have had some business with Sameer importing his art work."

"Why would Sameer kidnap Delong's girls?" Catherine asked. The more Petrov lied, the more she was sure he was.

"I don't know. I didn't even know he knew Alexi until he took the girls. I had seen them at the funeral, of course. Then at the warehouse."

"Why were you at the warehouse?"

"I was there to meet with Sameer about the crates of antiquities I had just imported for him. When I saw the girls, I was shocked!"

"Did you ask him why he had kidnapped them?"

"Yes, he said to force their mother to give him something her husband had stolen from him. I didn't trust him not to hurt them, so I took them from him and ran to the airport, where we were ambushed. I thought it was Sameer, but then I realized it was you and your people."

"Why did you run then if you knew it was us?"

"You shot my men and would have shot me, as well. So, I ran to save my life. I couldn't get to the girls, but I knew you wouldn't harm them."

Catherine let that comment slide.

"How did you happen to meet Barb and take her south after J.J."

"I saw her on the street and asked if she wanted a drive. She got in my car and told me about J.J. and how Ron, Alexi, had stolen money from Sameer. I offered to help her follow J.J with my jet and she said yes. I think I fell in love with her at the funeral, but it would have been disrespectful to ask her out then. The hours we spent together in the jet made me sure I wanted her in my life. I could understand how Alexi was so enamored of her. I didn't know then how he had treated her. I would have killed him myself if I had known. Still, he was my brother and we had been close as children. After Chernobyl, we had both been very ill for years. I almost died. Alexi had gone to America before I was well again and we lost touch. I moved here in 2008 with my import/export business. I didn't know he was here in Toronto."

"None of this has anything to do with Barb's disappearance! I have told you everything I know. All these questions are about Sameer. Why? Do you know something I don't? Sameer is dead, right?"

"We believe he is still alive. If he took Barb, what would be his motive?" Asked Catherine. She had spotted several holes in his story. "Do you think he is still after the money? Does he still think Barb knows where the money is?"

"I don't know what he believes, but if he is still after the money, Barb will be in grave danger, because she doesn't know anything about it."

Catherine looked at Slade. Neither believed him, but his concern for Barb seemed real. Catherine's cell vibrated in her pocket. After she spoke with Chuck, she put her hand to her forehead where a headache was forming. She had promised Barb she would keep her and the girls safe and she had failed. Again. Her men had just reported the girls were missing from their apartment. None of her surveillance team had been killed this time, which was good and that told her that Sameer didn't take them.

"Was that about her girls? Does he have them, too?" Petrov seemed to be really upset. Either he was a consummate actor or he didn't have Barb or her girls.

Slade realized that Catherine was feeling guilty and he had to get her back to her professional self, so she could think more analytically. He moved to rest his hand on her shoulder, but she moved away before he could. It would not have been professional. She moved to the window outlooking the city for just a moment. When she turned back to them, her eyes had lost the fearful look they had had and were now hunting eyes.

Petrov looked at her and shifted in his seat. This was not the woman who was a friend to Barb. This was the agent who would do what it took to get her back and to bring in the men who threatened Barb and her children; but it was also the agent who would bring down any threat to the city by any means necessary. For the first time, Petrov felt fear of this woman.

Slade looked at Petrov. "You can leave now, Peter, but don't leave town. We will find Barb and the girls. Don't interfere. You could get them all killed if you do. Leave it to us. I want your word on this," he commanded.

"Alright, Detective Slade. You will call me the second you have them?"

"Yes, I will." Slade promised.

Slade and Catherine watched him leave the restaurant.

"He is leaving now. Don't take your eyes off him for a millisecond." He commanded two of his agents. "What do you think, Catherine?"

"He has them. He put on an excellent performance. I almost believed him. He really has the 'don't look at me, I'm innocent' thing down pat. But the big question is, if Petrov has them, why this charade? Plus, I am positive he knows Sameer is alive and his story has so many holes in it, it looks like swiss cheese. For example, he wasn't just driving down the street and picked up Barb to go after J.J. Was he following Barb or J.J? And how did he know Ron was 'enamored' of Barb? Did Ron tell him? If so, he knew and spoke to Ron before the murder. Petrov knows his story won't hold up and yet, he doesn't seem to care. Why, I wonder? All those questions are important, but I really want to know if Barb is in on this. And what in God's name is 'this'? Slade, I feel like we are on a ticking bomb that is going off any second."

Slade stared at her. She was beautiful, smart, tenacious, protective and right now she was scared for her friend and her family. However, behind all that, her brain was correlating everything that had happened up to this point and accepting and rejecting theories and facts.

"Ok, Slade. If we accept the possibility that Barb and her kids are not in danger right now, that Petrov has them, what could the effects of this charade be? First, the restaurant could be closed for at least twenty-four to thirty-six hours as it is the crime scene, but probably only twenty-four hours as the twenty-third is a big night here with the Mayor and his guests, including the Russian Ambassador. They are taking over the entire place for the evening."

When Slade looked at her with his brows raised, she replied, "The notification was in my inbox this morning. The Russian Ambassador, could he be the target? No, I cannot see Sameer and his group going after the Ambassador. If anything, he would be an ally with Iran. We are missing something." Catherine was frowning as her mind searched for answers.

"I agree," said Slade. "If this landmark was destroyed, it would show how vulnerable we really are. That would be part of Sameer's motive. There could even be other attacks in other cities at the same time, coordinated to cause panic. To bring down this building correctly would require properly placed bombs. With all the commotion here tonight, they could have been set already. We need to bring in the bomb squad to search every inch of this place."

"Yes, we are going to need a lot of people and dogs...oh, no, Max! I'll have to go get her when I go home or get someone to pick her up and bring her to the office. I have Barb's key, so they can get in to get her." It was going to be a long night.

Petrov was on his way to Barb in the limo. Everything was going well. Barb's kidnapping was a diversion for the police, to focus on her and to leave the door open for Petrov to get what he wanted. Sameer wouldn't be able to put his plan in action until late on the twenty-third and he would need to be there front and center. If he got caught, all the better. He would never talk to the authorities. They would assume he was the leader behind the whole plan and he would want to take responsibility for the attack. He would take the blame for it all and if Sameer failed, Petrov had a backup plan. The Ambassador would not leave the building alive. Now Petrov was almost to the finish line of the biggest deal he had ever bartered and he couldn't lose this one. He wouldn't. It meant his freedom in so many ways.

Sameer watched the police scurrying like ants around the building from the cover of the parking garage across the street. What was Petrov doing? He wouldn't be able to get near the place now. He pulled his phone out, put the battery back in it and called him.

"What has happened, Petrov? What are the police doing there?"

"Someone kidnapped Barb! Was it you, Sameer? If you hurt her, I will kill you!"

"I did not take her! You are going to ruin everything! How do we get everything in place with the police in there?" Sameer was furious. He had never trusted Petrov. He seemed weak to him. He didn't know what it took to complete the mission, the determination, the belief in the cause, even if it meant your life. Petrov was so enamored with Delong's wife to the point where he would compromise the mission. If he did, Sameer would kill him and the woman himself.

"Calm yourself, Sameer. The police will leave by the morning of the twenty-third. The mayor and his guests will all be attending a big celebration that night. With all the deliveries and staff there getting ready for them, you will have no problem. They will all be rushed to get everything ready because the police are there now preventing them from doing their jobs. You will blend in with the uniforms I have provided for you and your men."

Sameer waited for Petrov to tell him what happened, but he didn't. "What happened to your woman, Petrov?"

"Don't worry about it, Sameer. I am taking care of that. You just get your men ready. Make sure they can perform this operation with their eyes closed."

"Don't you worry about my men, Petrov. They know what is at stake and will give their lives for the cause."

Petrov hung up and thought, they will have to.

When he arrived at the safe house where Barb was being kept, she was waiting for him in a fury.

"Where are my girls, Peter? You said I would see them!"

"I said you could call them and you can also see them on Skype. Come here and I will show you." Petrov opened his laptop and Barb saw the girls on the screen.

"How are you girls? Are my men treating you well? You are safe with them and will be home soon. Here is your mother." Peter stepped back so Barb could be in front of the screen.

"Are you guys ok?" asked the worried mother.

"We are fine. Are you ok, Mom?" they said in unison.

"Yes, I am fine, girls."

"What is going on, Mom?" asked Sarah.

"I don't know. Peter said it was to keep us all safe."

"Safe from what?" Sarah was the tenacious one.

Petrov admired that in her. He stood behind their mother. She looked at him over her shoulder. He put his arms around her and she let him. The twins' eyes opened wide. They had never seen their mother in a relationship with a man and their father didn't count as he had never showed any affection to their mom.

Peter looked down at her and said, "Sameer isn't dead and until he is, I will keep you safe."

Barb trembled in his arms.

"It will be alright, Zina. You are here with me and my men won't let him near you. This will all be over soon."

"How do you know that, Peter?" Barb was a strong, independent woman; and as harsh and uncaring as Ron had been, she had had to be, but even though in Peter's arms she felt safe, she would always question what she faced in life.

"In my line of work, I sometimes have had to deal with less than exemplary people. Sameer is one of them. Your friends Catherine and Detective Slade are close to capturing him. When they do, you will be safe again and can continue with your lives. Until then I will guard you. Don't worry, girls. I will protect your mother, too. Now do you need anything? Are you being treated well? Just tell my men what you want and they will get it for you. I need to talk to your mother, but she can call you whenever she wants. I can't tell her where you are, because of security, but that will only be for another forty-eight hours. Then we will all be together. We will talk to you again soon. Dasvidanja."

Petrov disconnected the link and turned to Barb. "I need to tell you something. Please listen to me and keep an open mind. Da?" he took her hands in his.

"Alright." Barb wasn't sure she wanted to hear what he had to say, but knew it was important enough for him to be nervous about telling her. Barb knew he was nervous about what he had to tell her because he was slipping into Russian.

"I was born in the Ukraine, which was part of Russia at one time. I had a brother, Alexi, who was eleven months older than me; and since we were born in the same year, we were always in the same grade at school and we were very close. Our parents were physicists and worked at Chernobyl. In the 1986 nuclear disaster, they were killed immediately, as were so many others. The ones who survived the blast were not so lucky. Some died within weeks of a horrible death caused by the radiation; others lived for years before succumbing to cancers caused by the radiation. Alexi survived thyroid cancer and later moved to New York to live with distant relatives who helped him finish his business degree.

"I wasn't so lucky. I almost died of leukemia. It took a long time for me to recover. By then I had lost touch totally with Alexi. I moved here in 2008 to expand the import/export business I had in St. Petersburg. One day last year I was at a conference for business men in Toronto and there he was, Alexi, or as you knew him, Ron Delong."

Barb gasped and tried to pull her hands free from Petrov. He held tight.

"He had changed his looks a lot and I almost didn't recognize him, but he knew me first. He had lost all his hair and was much thinner than I, but it was his eyes. Eyes don't change. We agreed to meet later the next day. I left immediately and put one of my men to work to find out everything he could about Ron Delong. Ron was in some very shady deals, but always kept just within the law, until he became emmeshed in Sameer's deal. I tried to interfere, but Alexi was working his own scam and when he stole Sameer's money, I knew it was just a matter of time. Sameer and his kind play for keeps and have no humanity in them. Killing is born in them. I wasn't fast enough and Sameer killed him before I could stop him that night. Just before he died, he said that you had the money. And Barb, he grinned when he said it, knowing that Sameer was going to kill him.

When I went to his funeral and saw you, I couldn't believe he would do something so spiteful to such a beautiful woman, his wife. I knew I had to scare you into giving me the money or Sameer would kill you or the girls, most probably take the girls to force you to give him the money. I have been trying to protect you from him all this time.

I fell in love with you the first time I saw you at the funeral. Yes, I know it was unseemly at my brother's service, but I wanted to protect you from Alexi's spite and Sameer's fanaticism. I know my business affairs have sometimes been on the other side of shady, but I have never killed anyone and I will keep you, Sarah and Kara safe with my last breath."

Petrov stared into Barb's eyes. There he saw surprise, confusion and dare he hope, love or at least understanding and acceptance. For the past three months, he had tried to get close to her, sometimes for only minutes at contrived casual meetings; sometimes for coffee at her house, and sometimes for longer periods of time at dinner. But it was on the plane that they spent the most time due to the altitude where she couldn't escape him.

They had talked, constrained at first, but with each subsequent meeting they had started to recognize each other's character. He saw

Barb's love for her girls, her friends, and even her company that her father had entrusted in her hands. Alexi had hurt her over and over again until he had killed any love she had had for him. His dying breath had been spent putting a target on her back. Had he killed any trust she could have in him, Peter, or any man for that matter, but especially for him? Would she trust that he was not like Ron, his own brother? Could he prove his love to her? He was going to try, but first, he had to make sure she was safe.

Sameer had found someone else to fund his upcoming terrorist act, so he wasn't totally focused on getting the money or revenge on Barb, yet. Petrov knew who that was and he would no longer be a problem after tomorrow. The Russian Ambassador would not be helping terrorists by funding their munitions and supplies. The CIA was paying Petrov a lot of money to see him eliminated; but it was the fact that he was out of their control if he finished this. He would no longer work for them. And if Sameer survived after the twenty-third, he might come after Barb out of spite, but Petrov didn't plan on letting him survive the night.

Barb gently placed her hand on his face. "I know you are not like Ron. He would have let Sameer have me and he wouldn't have cared what he did to me. Ron proved that with his dying breath. Plus, you saved my girls. For that reason alone, I will trust you and to me trust is more important than love."

Petrov folded her into his arms and sighed. He had her trust. That was sufficient for now. He had to finish the job and then he would take them away from people like Sameer and the life he had led. He was tired of the subterfuge, the constant looking over his shoulder. He wanted a life with Barb and her girls. He had enough money to provide them with everything they needed or wanted.

His job was to eliminate the Russian Ambassador, who was working with a terrorist group to bring down targets in Canada in tandem with other cells in the United States.

He had his men in place to make sure Sameer was killed before he could detonate the bombs to bring down the Tower. The bombs Petrov's men would place in the Tower were of a small load to cause chaos and panic.

The real plan would then evolve in the restaurant where the Ambassador was sitting. They also had an assassin in place as a female waiter, who would shoot him in the head, if need be. Her gun had a silencer and she would take advantage of the chaos to make the kill shot without anyone seeing her do it and getting away in the panic following the explosion. No one was to get hurt except the Ambassador, but there might be collateral damage and that was acceptable to the people who authorized this event.

This whole plan seemed too extravagant to just assassinate one man, and it was. The plan was to take out Sameer's whole cell and Sameer had helped him do it by killing five of his own men when he tried to make it appear as if he was murdered on the dock. Then he had brought in the rest of his men from the

States to finish the job and Petrov was going to make sure Sameer and his cell would all be eliminated or captured on the twenty-third.

Petrov was starting to believe his own cover. He had been an import/export dealer in Russia when the CIA had approached him to work for them. His business was a perfect cover and introduced him to some very unsavory characters. When the CIA asked him to move to Canada, he accepted their offer as it was getting dangerous to operate in Russia. Now he wanted out to build a life with Barb. Somewhere warm, somewhere he could enjoy life without looking over his shoulder all the time. He just had to finish this job. His life had been like living in the shadows for a long time, not quite real and not quite honest. Now he wanted a real life out of the shadows and into the sun.

Barb could hear Peter's heart beat as she hugged him with her ear on his chest. She pondered how life could be so serendipitous at times. Should she believe Peter? She wanted to. She, who was always so by-the-book, never do anything spur of the moment, wanted to toss aside her whole life and go with Peter. She would leave her friends, her business that was her legacy from her father, and … and what? She would have her girls and Peter.

Peter was the catalyst. He was the one she would share a life with, who said he loved her. Yes, it was fast, so unlike anything she would normally do. She wanted more from life than constant worry over work, making mortgage payments, and paying for the girls' university, although that was a labor of love. She wanted them to be able to do what they loved and go where they wanted to in life. She wanted more than to do what everyone expected her to do. She was lonely and had been for a very long time. She wanted to be loved and cared for. And she felt she could be by Peter, maybe. He protected her and the girls and she liked that. But could she trust him? Would he want to take over her whole life? Would she have to answer to him? Would he try to control her?

She had fixed the problem at her firm. She wanted to protect her father's good name, so she gave back the twenty million Ron had stolen. Now she could sell out to any one of her competitors and make enough money to buy a place in the sun. There were already offers on the table for her firm. She could make a new life for herself, maybe a life with Peter. The girls could finish their degrees and make their lives into what they wanted. They wouldn't be constricted to what they could do by what it cost. Money would not control who and what they could be, like it had her. Nor would any man.

Barb knew that if she told Peter about the money, she would again be under a man's rule. He would never let her be free of him and she needed to be free more than anything in her life. It was like a disease, first her father, then her husband. And though she was a successful woman, owning her own firm, making great money, she had been constantly aware of the fact that she could lose it all by Ron's actions. Now that he was gone, she was free of him and she needed to be free. She was never going back.

Catherine by Evonne D. Haley

Chapter 37

On the twenty-third of December, Sameer stood in the warehouse scrutinizing the munitions for the job. Everything looked good; they had enough to bring down the building. He had the news release set to be sent to the newspapers declaring who was responsible, for all the glory, to show these infidels that they weren't safe in their homes or on their streets; that they were not invincible to terrorism. Their complacent attitude would be shaken to their roots and their proximity to the United States would not keep them safe. And it would all be done in the name of Allah.

Sameer had not forgotten about Delong and his money, the money that Delong had stolen from the cause, that he said with his dying breath his wife had in her possession. She denied it, but Sameer knew she had it and he was going to make her an example for others who would try to steal from him and the cause. He also wanted to get back at Petrov for he had protected the woman and her seed. He couldn't reach the woman's spawn; they

317

were too well protected, but he could get to the woman. Petrov would die tonight along with her.

The yellow police tape was laying on the ground. Workers trampled it under their feet as they hurried to and from unloading food and supplies. The water man had a dolly for the two hundred bottles of water being delivered as did the produce man unloading cases of potatoes, lettuce, mushrooms and other vegetables for this night's gala. The meat supplier was impatiently waiting for his turn in the elevator to bring in the porter house steaks, prime rib, seafood, pork and other fare for the guests tonight. The electrician and his crew were also waiting to get up to the restaurant to look at a circuit breaker that seemed to be malfunctioning. The four elevators, two for authorized personnel and two for guests, were constantly moving up and down as the busy workers were trying to do their jobs. The fifth elevator was not working and had a crew trying to correct the problem as quickly as possible. The cleaning crew were very frustrated as they tried to clean the restaurant and lobby with so many people trampling everything and everyone in their path to complete their jobs.

It was chaos, total chaos. Sameer was wound up like a jack in the box. The men with him were not sure what would go off first, Sameer or the bombs, and no one wanted to cross him. Posing as the electrician and his crew, Sameer had access to the entire building. He spread his men throughout it to perform their tasks. No one paid any attention to them.

Because of the police investigation into the kidnapping of Barb Delong, the entire building had been off limits to everyone, including staff, delivery men, maintenance crews, etc. Now they were all trying to catch up on their duties, plus there were extra people trying to get ready for tonight's black-tie event. As long as you looked like someone who should be there, had the right uniforms and work orders, no one questioned you beyond a cursory inspection. Sameer had parked the electrician's van close to the building on the maintenance access road to the south. Its logo told everyone who they were supposed to be.

Two hours later Sameer's men were finished. Everything was timed to go off at ten o'clock that evening. Now Sameer just had one more task and that was to get the Delong woman. If she wouldn't give him the money, his money, she would be an uninvited guest at the ten o'clock show. That money was for the cause and without it they had had to revamp the job to a much smaller event. It would still be an eye opener and complete the job of showing this city of over four million people and the rest of this country that they weren't safe. Nobody was safe from the power of ISIS.

Sameer's man, who he had following Petrov, reported that he and his woman were at a house downtown. Sameer's men were going to get her and take her to the warehouse he had rented just for this mission to house all his men and their equipment.

"What about Petrov? He's there with her. He will try to stop us." Sameer's man asked.

"If he interferes, and I hope he will, take him as well. If he resists too strongly, kill him." Sameer was in charge. His word was law. His men, however, were beginning to question his leadership. He wasn't focused on the job. He was obsessing about the woman. There was no reasoning with him and he was going to sabotage the mission. They were supposed to get in, do the job, and get out.

"But Petrov is connected with some powerful people."

"Do you question me?" Sameer roared.

"No, we will get the woman."

There was no reasoning with him so they just prayed to Allah that they would succeed with the mission. Sameer saw that his men were not like those in his homeland. They questioned him and his strategy, even his actions. They were supposed to comply immediately upon his commands. They had spent too much time in the United States and had taken on some of their propaganda, thinking for themselves. Not good. Maybe he would have to eliminate them. It would be easy to get rid of them after they had taken care of Petrov and the woman. He had already eliminated his first team to take the heat off after the fiasco of kidnapping the Delong females. The girls had seen his men and him, so he had staged their deaths and his fake one. As far as he knew the police thought he was dead so they wouldn't be looking for him and his new team.

"Never mind, I am going with you." Sameer informed his men. "I want it done right this time."

■■

Petrov had four men outside the safe house and two inside with him and Barb. He really thought Sameer would attempt to take Barb. He knew his men were not necessarily a deterrent either. Sameer was a radical. He would go to the max to accomplish his mission. Sameer also showed a sociopathic trait when it came to the money. He had fixated on Barb after Ron's final knife to Barb's gut. He didn't understand Ron's hatred of the woman. She was just a woman, not worth anything. Get rid of her, fill the landfill with more of them. They weren't worth the energy to hate or dwell on. Therefore, Ron must have been telling the truth; she had the money. Petrov didn't know if she did, but he didn't care. He had millions, plenty to live a rich, comfortable life with Barb.

His watch started vibrating on his wrist. No noise to alert anyone, but him. His men outside had seen something to put them on guard. He put his finger to his lips telling Barb not to speak and took her hand to pull her down the hall. He wanted her out of the line of fire and he didn't want Sameer to get within arms reach of her. He keyed in the code for the panic room where they would stay until his men came to get them out after the all clear was given. If his men didn't come, there was another way out of the building from the panic room, a one-way tunnel that only opened from the inside.

Petrov held Barb in his arms as he waited for the all clear. He knew she was afraid and he tried to calm her fears, but to tell the truth, he was afraid as well. If Sameer's men got past his men, they had no defense left except the tunnel, which was alright, as long as Sameer didn't know about it. Petrov was worried, because Sameer shouldn't have known about the safehouse. If he could find out that information, he could know about the tunnel. As Petrov waited, he watched the screens showing the outside areas of the property as Sameer's men decimated his own and forced their way into the house. The inside cameras documented the all-out savagery of Sameer's men as they tore their way through his men.

Suddenly Sameer's face filled the screen and he said, "Come out, Petrov, with the woman and I will let you live. I just want the money and I know she has it. If she gives it up to me, you can both go free. I will give you one minute; and if you don't come out, I will blow this house apart."

324

Catherine by Evonne D. Haley

Peter stared into Barb's eyes and then kissed her lips. "Ok, Sameer. Give us just a minute."

He led the way into the tunnel, pulling her along. He prayed they were ignorant of at least this one detail about the safe house. At the end of the tunnel was a steel door with a retinal scanner.

Barb was shaking. She knew if Peter opened the door, there was a good chance Sameer or his men could be on the other side. She also knew they wouldn't kill her immediately, although she would soon pray for that. Peter, however, might be expendable.

Suddenly the tunnel seemed to implode on itself. The percussion hurt her ears and made her nauseous. They had blown the door of the panic room. Peter let the reader scan his eyeball and the door slid into the wall. Sunlight blinded her for a moment, but Peter pulled her through and ran for the SUV parked in the ally. They never made it. Sameer's men were all around them with weapons aimed at them from every direction.

"So, it has to be this way then," said Sameer. He almost looked happy and probably was. He had a sadistic streak in him that anticipated torturing the woman. He grabbed Barb's arm and forced her into a sedan, then turned to Peter, "We won't need you anymore," and climbed into the sedan.

One of Sameer's men aimed and fired directly into Petrov's chest. As he fell to the ground, he saw an upside-down view of legs as they moved to their vehicles and drove away. He had failed and now Sameer would hurt her. His men were probably all dead or severely injured. He had no option, but to try to get to Catherine or Slade. They would do what needed to be done to get Barb back, but first he had to stay alive long enough to tell them.

Two very small legs stopped beside him. "I called 911, mister. They are coming." Then the little boy ran away. Peter could hear the sirens getting louder as they got closer. He had to stay awake long enough to tell them where to find Barb.

First, the police came and then the paramedics moved in. He grabbed the hands trying to help him tightly.

"Call Detective Slade. They will kill her." Peter wheezed.

The paramedic trying to get his hand free finally yelled, "Somebody call Detective Slade," and then more softly to Peter, "He will come to the hospital. Let me help you so you can talk to him there."

"Make sure...Slade ... help Barb..." Peter's hands fell to his sides.

He could hear the sirens and feel them working on his chest trying to stop the bleeding; and then he saw the bright florescent lights and the white tiled ceiling as they rushed him into the trauma center at the hospital. He closed his eyes against the glare of the lights.

Suddenly, Slade was leaning over him, "I'm here, Peter. What happened?"

Catherine by Evonne D. Haley

"He has her. Wants the money. Will kill her. Tonight. at ten at..Tower." His eyes closed again.

Catherine was there when he opened them again.

"Peter, it's Catherine. Can you talk to me?"

He tried to open his eyes. He was in a room with tubes in his arms and other places and an oxygen mask was on his face. Machines beeped. He tried to push the mask off so he could talk, but his arms weren't working.

"It's Ok, Peter," Catherine took the mask off. "There, is that better?"

He tried to say yes, but his mouth was too dry. She put a straw in his mouth so he could drink some water. It seemed to evaporate in his mouth before it reached his throat, but he finally got some down.

"Better?" she asked and he nodded.

"Can you tell me what happened?"

328

Catherine by Evonne D. Haley

"Sameer has Barb. I tried to protect her, but he killed all my men and he thinks I am dead, too, probably." His voice was shaking.

"It's Ok, Peter. Take your time. Do you know where he took her?"

Catherine wanted to pull the information she needed right out of his head, but she spoke calmly and slowly to him, knowing she couldn't rush it.

Peter knew telling her the information she needed to save Barb would ruin the assassination planned for tonight, but he didn't care. All he wanted was to get Barb back safely. He tried to wet his lips and Catherine was there with more water.

"Here, Peter, sip slowly."

"He's going to blow up the Tower at ten o'clock tonight. Has bombs set already. He will take her there. It will be symbolic to kill her there. The money was for a big event, but he couldn't get it in time, so he is taking down a landmark to show he can do it. I hope she is still alive. He is cruel and will torture her.

329

Please save her, Catherine. I tried, but I failed her." His eyes were closing.

Chapter 38

Barb's arms were numb. They were tied behind her and her mouth was taped with duct tape. She wished everything was numb. She was very cold. Peter was dead. She had seen them shoot him. They were going to kill her, too. Her face was swollen and she could feel blood running down her cheek. She could barely see through the slits in her eyes, the right one swollen nearly shut. Sameer didn't get what he wanted from her and he was enraged. She tried to tell him she couldn't give him the money, but he refused to believe her. So, he beat her. She had at least two broken ribs, three broken fingers, burn marks all over her body, a broken nose and two missing teeth; all she could recover from, but not the next injury he had planned for her.

She was now sitting beside a bomb. The red numbers on the timer were counting down the minutes. There was one hour and thirty minutes left. Sameer had told her he would let her live if she told him where the money was. Barb was not a stupid woman. She knew he would kill her anyway. Her girls were safe. Peter had made sure of that. His men had orders that they were to take the girls to Catherine if anything happened to him. They were probably there now. Sameer had threatened to kill them, too, but Catherine would go after Sameer with every resource she had to bring justice for Barb's death. The girls would be safe.

At this point, Barb was resigned to her death. No one knew she was here. She would die with all the others in the building. So be it. She did wish she had listened more to Catherine, Maggie and Ella about life after death. She hoped there was life after death. She had gone to church when she was young with her parents so she sort of believed in Christianity. But she had never lived her life as someone who believed in Christ or had Him as a living force in her life. She was not a bad person. She didn't cheat or lie on her taxes or murder anyone, although right now she prayed Sameer would fail tonight and get his comeuppance. He was evil and needed to be stopped; hopefully, before this bomb detonated. If only someone would come and disarm it. Or at the very least, get everyone out of this building.

"Please God," she prayed, "save all the innocent people in this building. They have families and loved ones they want to go home to tonight. Please don't let their children have to grow up without them. Amen."

She didn't pray for herself. It was too late for her. How did she get here? She had always been a quiet girl, like Tara. Always did what was expected of her. Her father had groomed her to take over the company, even though it was not what she had dreamed of doing. She had wanted to be a linguistic interpreter, traveling the world. She loved her father, but he had never really known her, not her or her dreams.

When she had met Ron, she had actually thought that maybe this was her way to a new life, but Ron had turned out to be a much more violent version of her father. Oh, she felt disloyal to even think that of her father, of comparing him with Ron.

Then she met Peter. And, again, he was the same. He wanted her for his desires. He didn't know her at all, nor did he want to. He saw her as what he wanted. Well, she had done what she needed to do for herself and her girls. Too bad it was too late for her, but not her girls. She had made sure of that.

The door to the corner of the Tower base opened and Sameer entered, blinking his eyes trying to adjust to the darkness. He came over to Barb, ripping the duct tape off her mouth. He noted the timer. It was down to twenty minutes.

"Will you tell me where the money is now, woman?" he asked her for the last time.

"If I said yes, would you let all the people in this building live? Would you stop the bomb?" she asked him instead.

Catherine by Evonne D. Haley

He looked at her. She was a mess. Her face was so bruised, he could hardly recognize her, but that didn't matter, because she wouldn't live past the next twenty minutes.

She read the answer in his eyes. There would be no mercy from him for her or anyone else. She closed her eyes to shut out his face.

Sameer turned to leave and stepped to the door. He only had about fifteen minutes to get clear of the blast area. He glanced at the timer and then paused. There was something wrong. It still read twenty minutes, just as it did when he entered.

"What have you done?" he screamed at her as the door was jerked open and men grabbed him, forcing him down on his face to the floor and then roughly handcuffing him. Before they took him out, he stared at Barb with such hate in his eyes that she shook with fear.

Catherine and Slade came in and knelt down by Barb.

"The ambulance is here for you, honey," Catherine was being as gentle as she could be with Barb. She was so battered, she didn't dare touch her, let alone move her.

Two paramedics came with a backboard to carry her out to the ambulance.

"We will triage her in the bus," one of the paramedics said to Catherine as they got her strapped on the board. "We are taking her to University Hospital," he said as they carried her out.

Catherine took her hand on the way to the ambulance.

"I will be there with you, Barb. Everything's alright. We have the girls. They are safe. And you will be fine." She let go of her hand and stepped back. The doors were shut and the sirens started before they left the scene.

"You go, Catherine. I'll finish up here." Slade knew she wanted to be there with her very resilient friend. They also both knew that Barb's immediate statement was crucial to convict Sameer of his crimes and she was one of the only ones left alive to give them that information. If Peter had not given them the information in time to disarm the bombs, many people would have died including Barb and the Ambassador. Slade was actually quite surprised that Peter told them about the hit on the Ambassador. There would be a lot of angry people about that, which meant Peter could be on a hit list himself now. Slade would get Chuck to look into that.

Slade had over fifty police officers to lock down the Tower and everything in a thousand-foot radius, plus thirty CSIS agents to contain the immediate site, and the bomb squad as well as Chuck's military intelligence crew. There was going to be an enormous amount of paper work to be completed and an equal amount of egos who wanted to claim this coup for the advancement of their careers.

"How are you doing, brother?" asked Chuck.

"Tired but good. No one died and no one got blown up. A very good evening altogether."

"Why don't you go to the hospital to see Catherine? I can oversee events here, now." Offered Chuck.

"In a little bit, I will. I see some big wigs coming this way. I need to deal with them first." Sighed Slade.

"Ok, you can deal with them. Have fun." Laughed Chuck as he moved off to take care of one of the million facets to a crime scene.

Chapter 39

Slade walked wearily into University Hospital Trauma Center. One of the guards came over.

"You are looking for Agent Henley, Slade?"

"Yeah, Mark, I am."

"She's down the hall in Trauma 3. Did someone really try to blow up the Tower?"

"Yes, but they failed, Mark. We won this time."

Slade was so tired. He had spent six hours at the crime scene and two more talking to the brass about whose crime scene it was or wasn't. Director Blanchette used the might of his power and convinced them all that this was part of the task force investigation, so it was finally decided it was theirs. They would be writing reports for weeks with all the T s crossed and i s dotted so there would be no technicality that Sameer could use to wiggle his way out of a conviction. Barb would be their star witness.

As he turned the corner, he saw Catherine sitting in the hall holding the hands of Barb's daughters, who were quietly crying.

"I want you to know she looks terrible, so bruised, but those bruises will fade and the swelling will go down. The doctors are taking very good care of her." Catherine was trying to prepare the girls for the first time they would see their mother.

"You won't leave us, will you Catherine?" asked Kara.

"No, honey, I will stay with you," Catherine hugged her. Then she looked up and saw Slade. She spoke softly to the girls and stood up to come to him. He opened his arms and she stepped into them.

"How are you all doing?" he asked gently.

"We're good. Just tired. You look tired, too, Jeremy. Did they leave the case with us?"

"Yes, we are in charge of it and have a lot of work to finish it. How's Barb?"

Catherine by Evonne D. Haley

Catherine walked him down the hall out of earshot of the twins.

"They had to operate to remove her spleen and stop the internal bleeding. That was the worst. She has four broken ribs, a broken wrist, three broken fingers, cigarette burns on her body and her nose was broken. She has multiple hematomas. He tortured her, Jeremy. I have never seen anyone beaten so badly who lived." She leaned into him for his strength.

The nurse in charge came to speak to Catherine. "They are taking her to post op care on the fourth floor, Catherine. There is a family room there where you all can wait until we get her settled. The doctors will speak to you there."

"Thank you, Betty. I will be there with her girls." Catherine and Slade were well known at the hospital due to the violent nature of their jobs.

Both girls stood up when they saw Betty and came down the hall to Catherine. "Was that about Mom?"

"Yes. We are going to the fourth floor where she is being settled into her room. We will have to wait a bit until the doctor comes to speak to us, but it shouldn't be long."

Slade hugged each of the twins. "I'm sorry about your Mom, girls, but she is a very strong lady. We are all praying for a quick recovery. How are you two doing? Do you need anything?"

They looked at each other, then at him, "No, we're fine," they both said at once.

As soon as they settled the girls into the family room, the surgeon and the attending physician came in to speak with them. The girls both stood holding hands.

"We removed her spleen, wrapped her ribs, set her broken bones, but we had some problems stopping the internal bleeding. We gave her two litres of blood and we will be watching her closely for the next twenty-four to forty-eight hours. I believe she will recover fully barring any complications. Mostly, she needs rest, so only two visitors at a time for

342

only ten minutes every hour. We will see how she is in the next few hours. Now, you two young ladies need your rest in order to be here for her, so eat and sleep, here if you want."

"Yes, we want to be here; thank you, Doctor," said Sarah.

As the doctor left the room, Slade followed him out leaving Catherine and the girls with the attending physician.

"Dr. Sinclair," Slade touched his arm and he turned. Slade had his badge out. The doctor nodded and stopped.

"Were there any injuries you didn't inform her family of that I need for forensics in this case?" Slade spoke softly.

"Yes, there is a rape kit for you at the nurses' station. Dr. Reuben, the attending physician, can give you more information on that. I only knew about it, because it was preventing me from attending to my patient in surgery." He paused. "I have never seen anyone that badly beaten other than in a car accident. It is hard to believe a human being

343

would do that to another human being let alone a woman. I hope you caught him, Detective." He walked down the hall to handle the next trauma patient.

Slade turned back to the family room. Dr. Reuben was explaining what the next few hours would entail for Barb.

"She will have some pain, but we are giving her pain medication through her IVs as well as some nutrients. She will only be able to eat soft foods for a few days. Her bruising will look worse before it gets better, but it will get better, girls. She is through the worst of it."

A nurse came to the door and nodded to the doctor.

"You can go in to see her now for ten minutes."

"Thank you, Doctor," the twins said as they hurried after the nurse.

"Ok, Sam," said Catherine. They had known each other for years and had dealt together with crime victims many times. "What did Dr. Sinclair leave out in front of the girls?"

Slade moved over to her side. He knew she would take this news hard, but she was intelligent and knew one of the first torture events for a woman was rape, sadistic, humiliating and painful rape.

"The kit and the report are in the box at the nurses' station and there is plenty of DNA evidence that will help you in this case. She will need counselling to get through this. Her twins are young and they will probably need help recovering from this as well. Also, as she was coming out of anesthetic, she kept saying a man's name, 'Peter'. She was very agitated. Is he the one who did this to her?"

"No, he tried to save her and got shot, which she saw. He is up on the ICU, hopefully, recovering. I need to tell him she is going to be alright and Catherine can speak with Barb when she is more coherent."

Catherine by Evonne D. Haley

Slade knew Catherine was upset, but she was a professional agent and knew how to appear calm, even when she wanted to scream in frustration and anger.

"Well, I have more patients to see." Dr. Reuben patted Catherine's shoulder as he left.

"Are you ok, Cat?" Slade was a little concerned.

She wasn't moving or saying anything. Her eyes were closed. She was trying to pray, but she couldn't decide what to pray for when all she could think was, 'why? God, why?' She knew she was reacting to all the stress and that it was her friend in there, hurt physically, mentally and emotionally, perhaps scarred for life.

"I'm Ok, Jeremy. Let's go take a statement from Peter if we can. Oh, here are the girls back."

Both girls collapsed in her arms sobbing. Catherine knew this was coming after they saw their mother.

"Oh, my God! I couldn't recognize her, Catherine. I asked the nurse if we had the wrong room. I can't believe it's Mom. Is she going to live? There are tubes and stuff stuck in her everywhere!" Kara broke down again sobbing. Sarah never said a word, just hugged Catherine, crying.

"I know she looks bad, but she will recover, girls. She will need your support and that means you will need to take care of her, see that she gets the rest she will need to get better, for her body to heal and patience and understanding while her mind heals. That will take longer. We will take one day at a time. OK?"

Sarah spoke up, "But you will be here, right, Catherine?"

"Yes, for the next two to three days, I will be here with you. I can work some from here so I can be with you until your Mom is more alert and feeling better. After you take her home, I will be around and I can run up to see you whenever I'm home. I won't desert you."

Catherine hugged them both. "I have to go up to see Peter in the ICU for just a few minutes. Why don't you two go the cafeteria and get something to eat or at least a drink. You can't see your mom again for another forty minutes or so and you need to keep up your strength. I will meet you back here when I am done."

They both nodded and headed to the elevators. They were close and would be good support for each other.

Peter Petrov was in Surgical Critical Care, a ward that was kept exceedingly clean and required masks, gowns, booties, and gloves for all visitors and staff. He was going in and out of consciousness, agitated, saying Barb's name. The nurse in charge stopped Catherine and Slade at the nurse's station.

"We need him to calm down some. Do you know who 'Barb' is, 'Catherine?"

"Yes, he needs to know she is safe. He was trying to keep her safe when he was shot. Can we talk to him for a few minutes?" She asked.

"Yes, if that will calm him, that would be the very best thing you can do for him right now, but I will only give you five minutes."

"Ok, thanks," Catherine said as she headed into Peter's room.

He was hooked to machines that were beeping and had tubes inserted in his body to keep him hydrated and to feed him pain medication and antibiotics, as well as drainage tubes and heart and lung monitors.

Catherine went over to his side and leaned down to talk to him.

"Peter, can you hear me? I have news of Barb."

Peter stirred agitatedly, moving his head from side to side. Then he opened his eyes.

"Hi, Peter. Barb is doing well. We got her out and disarmed all the bombs while we evacuated the building. Sameer is in custody and Barb and her girls are safe. You can stop worrying about them. Ok? You just need to get better."

Peter nodded his head as his eyes closed again, but he was calm now, not agitated.

Catherine turned to see who had come into the room. It was the surgeon, Dr. Sinclair. He looked at the monitors and took his stethoscope to hear Peter's heart and breathing sounds.

"Whatever you told him worked better than all the medication I could have given him and has really calmed him down."

"He was worried about Barb, his girlfriend. I told him she is safe and her family is safe. He just needed to know that, so he could stop worrying. How is he doing, Dr. Sinclair?"

"He is doing much better now. His heart rate is down as is his blood pressure. He is still having a lot of pain; but we are medicating him for that, as much as we can without affecting his heart rate. It is a juggling act in some ways. I expect to see him improve in the next few hours now. I didn't realize that Barb Delong was his girlfriend; so, if you are in the hospital, if you could come see him every couple of hours with good news for him, I expect to see him greatly improved within twenty-four hours."

"No problem. That is good news, Dr. Sinclair. We really need to talk to him; but we can wait until tomorrow, if he will be more coherent by then. I will be on the fourth floor with Barb and her girls for the next few days, so I will come up to check on him every couple of hours. We will need a formal statement from him as soon as we can to lock down this case."

"I wouldn't expect anything from him for at least twenty-four hours. I am on duty overnight, so I will be around the hospital and the nurses know how to reach me, if necessary." He patted Catherine's shoulder. "Get some rest yourself, Catherine." He said as he left the room.

"I need to go back to the girls now, Jeremy. Come with me and you can catch me up on tonight's events."

"Sure. You need to get some rest, Catherine, and so do the girls. Let's go see them and talk for a few minutes; then I want all of you to try to get some sleep, even if it is just a few hours. Ok?" Slade knew how tired he was and he didn't have the stress of having a close friend nearly beaten to death and the responsibility of caring for her two daughters.

"I won't fight you on this one, Jeremy, but you have to follow your own advice as well."

"I will, Cat, I promise. I am too tired to argue with you," he promised. Just then his cell phone started ringing. Then Catherine's. They looked at each other. This couldn't be good, not at five in the morning. They both answered and walked away from each other to hear the caller on the other end of the phone.

"Catherine speaking. Yes, Director Blanchette. Yes, Sir."

She turned to Slade as she hung up.

"He escaped? How is that even possible?"

Catherine by Evonne D. Haley

"You stay here with Barb and the girls. I will send more guards for them and for Peter as soon as I get to the station and I will explain to the Director that you were needed here until we have security in place. I'm sorry, Cat. You won't get any sleep tonight. Keep your phone on so I can reach you." He leaned in and kissed her, hard.

"Call me as soon as you get details." She reached up and put her hand on the side of his face. Memorizing his features. Then she watched as he ran for the elevator.

How in the world did Sameer escape? It should have been impossible, thought Catherine as she stopped outside the family room on the fourth floor.

Kara came out of the family room rubbing her eyes. "What's going on, Catherine?" Kara was the twin who didn't say much or show her feelings, but she was very intuitive.

Catherine paused with her mouth open. She watched Kara's eyes and knew she couldn't lie to her for her sake as well as Sarah's.

"Sameer has escaped. I wasn't going to tell you, but you need to know for you and Sarah to be alert in case he tries to get to your mother. I really don't think he will, because that would be a crazy thing for him to attempt. However, he has shown that he isn't totally sane. Slade has more guards coming, so we should be safe here. I will stay with you."

Sarah came out of the family room looking exhausted. "What's going on?"

"That fiend escaped. I am just so tired of him. Can we shoot him, if he comes here?" Kara was looking so serious, and then Catherine realized, she was. This had been a very stressful time for them all.

Catherine laughed, "Yes, if he shows up here, we can shoot him."

Kara turned back into the family room to make coffee, "Well, that's good."

Chapter 40

Slade walked into the conference room where the task force was hard at work at six o'clock in the morning.

"Do we have any idea of his location?" he asked Roger.

"He hasn't hit any bank machines yet, but we are searching through city, traffic and business cameras. If he's moving out there, we should get something soon. If he's gone to ground, it will take longer. If he tries to get out of the city, we will see him. However, if he's smart, he could change his appearance, use a wig, beard, makeup to change his facial structure, but I don't think he is that smart. Plus, our scanners can account for some modifications. He is the most wanted man in Canada and in the top ten in the US; someone will spot him and call it in."

"Ok, I have put twelve officers at the hospital with Catherine. I told them to place two each with Peter and Barb and the rest out of sight. Sameer is just crazy enough to try to get to Barb or Petrov. I almost hope he does. That would be the quickest way to end this." Slade was wiped out. He sat in one of the plush office chairs and leaned back. He would just close his eyes for a minute. The next thing he knew was Chuck touching his shoulder.

"Slade, wake up. We need you."

Slade opened his eyes to see a concerned Chuck leaning over him.

"What's up, Chuck?" He brushed his hands over his face trying to wipe away the fatigue.

"I am so sorry, Jeremy, but Catherine has disappeared from the hospital. She told the twins she was going up to check on Peter, but when she never came back, they alerted the guards. Apparently, she never made it to Peter's room. She's been gone for over an hour."

"I can't believe this. I should have stayed with them. We need to search the hospital from top to bottom. I will go organize that. I need you here, Chuck. Ask the two techies over there to hack into the hospital security cameras and find out where he took her. Yes, I said hack. We don't have time for red tape. Just do it. I will take the blame from the Director."

"Here, put this earwig in so we have constant communication." Roger was feeling guilt ridden and was as tired and frustrated as everyone else was. He should have made Catherine wear one when she left the crime scene at the Tower. Now all he could do was enforce it on Slade so they wouldn't lose him, too.

Guilt spread through Slade so deep he felt nearly crippled with it. Why had he come back here? Why didn't he stay with her? He knew Sameer would go after Peter or Barb, but he didn't think he would touch Catherine. Was she just the one he could reach? Or did he harbour hate against her because she got between him and Barb? Only God knew the answer to that. God, please keep Catherine safe; don't let anyone else get hurt by this man. Help me find them now.

Catherine by Evonne D. Haley

****

Catherine watched Sameer as he paced the room. He didn't have much space to pace in and that made him even more irate. She had at first tried to talk to him, but then she realized that he didn't hear her words, because she was a woman and her words didn't count. When he opened his overcoat, and showed her the bomb vest, she knew that he couldn't be reached. He didn't care if he died and he wanted to take as many people as he could with him, including her.

They were in a small conference room on the fourth floor. He hadn't taken her far. He wanted to take Barb out with them; his hatred of her knew no bounds. She had become his sole focus, the one who had ruined his plans and stopped him from completing his act of terrorism. It was almost inconceivable that a woman had done this to him.

Slade was hurrying into the hospital's back entrance when Roger tapped into his ear wig.

Catherine by Evonne D. Haley

"He has her on the fourth floor, just down the hall from Barb's room in the left wing. We went back an hour or so on the hospital's video surveillance and saw him take her in there. She has not attempted to take him down, because we believe he has a bomb strapped to his chest. He has a heavy overcoat on; and when he first approached her in the hall, he opened it. She then went with him willingly. We believe she was trying to get him out of the hospital, but he pushed her into the room they are in now. We are working on getting audio in the room through the hospital speaker system, and it should only be a few more minutes. I have informed the bomb squad and they are on their way to you now."

"Ok, thanks, Roger. I will wait here at the back entrance to the hospital for them. Patch me into the audio as soon as you get it."

"Sure, boss." Roger hung up.

Slade felt totally panicked. They were dealing with a fanatic, who had nothing to lose. His life meant nothing to him and neither did anyone else's. This was the worse case scenario for a police officer to walk into. When he was an officer on the force, getting a call for a domestic dispute was only one step down from this situation. Usually the perpetrator didn't have a bomb strapped to himself, but he often had a gun and threatened to kill his spouse, kids, or the police with it. Sameer was willing to kill a lot of innocent people and there was probably no way of talking him down.

That left the question of how to get Catherine out of there as well as all the patients in that section of the hospital or to get Sameer to come out on his own. Knowing Catherine, she had probably run all these scenarios though her head and was trying to come up with a plan.

Catherine had come up with a plan. Now, to get Sameer to go along with it.

"Sameer. I will take you to Barb."

He stopped pacing and stared at her.

Catherine by Evonne D. Haley

"Why would you do that?"

"Well, I know you are serious and I don't want anyone else in this hospital hurt. "

He stared at her for a minute. If she led him to Barb, then he would have them both in his power.

"No tricks." He commanded her.

She stood up slowly and started toward the door. She prayed Roger had seen what she had conveyed to him in sign language. She knew they would have tapped into video and audio feeds as soon as they found what room he had her in. She had kept her hands close to her lap so Sameer didn't notice. Now she had to get him into the unit that would hopefully, keep the casualties to a minimum.

Roger had caught the message from Catherine the last two times she had signed it. When she stood up, he reported, "They are on their way to the isolation unit, Slade." They all knew she could be going to her death as well as his. There would be no way for her to get out if he detonated the bomb with her inside.

Sameer kept hold of her jacket as she walked him down the corridor and into the next wing.

"Why is she in the isolation ward?" he asked when he saw the big doors to the unit.

"Because she was infected with radiation when they found her from the contaminates in the explosives."

"What contaminates? There were no contaminates. I would have been sick and so would my men."

"Well, you probably are. You just don't know it yet. It showed up in her blood work when she came in the hospital, probably because of all the cuts in her skin when she was sitting up against the bomb at the Tower."

"It doesn't matter. I just need her alive until she tells me where the money is."

"Here we are. We have to enter the first door and put on the gowns, masks, booties and

362

gloves before we can go through the second door."

"No, we don't. Get in there, now."

"We can only go in one at a time. The doors won't open until you have put on the isolation gear and push the red button. That will open the second door where Barb is kept. I will show you." Catherine started toward the door.

"No, you stay here. You want to get in first to warn somebody in there. I will go first and then you come in. I can see you through the glass and I can detonate this at any time if you try to run away."

Sameer stepped into the decontamination chamber and pushed the red button. He wasn't concerned about the gear he was supposed to put on. Both doors automatically locked leaving Catherine outside. Sameer's evil eyes glared at her as he realized she had tricked him. And then she saw him push the button on his vest. He was not going alone, or so he thought. Even with the blast proof doors protecting her, she felt the reverberation of the bomb exploding that shook the building and caused ceiling tiles to fall and dust to rain down on her head.

Slade ran to Catherine's side as she was picking herself up off the floor.

"I'm Ok, Slade, I'm Ok." She was shaken badly; but alive, thanks to the blast proof doors to the isolation unit and her quick thinking. Her message to Roger told him to get everybody out of that unit, which he did and to activate lock down of the unit when Sameer pushed the red button. Lock down of the unit automatically locked both doors so Sameer was caught between them. She wasn't sure of how much those doors could take, but it was better than letting Sameer activate the bomb anywhere else in the hospital. The doors were made to isolate contaminates from the rest of the hospital and the red button was a failsafe to totally shut down the unit. She also took the chance that he wanted to kill Barb more than her.

"Catherine, can you hear me?" Slade was talking to her but she couldn't hear him due to the percussion on her ears from the blast.

"I'm Ok, Slade. I just can't hear too well yet." She turned into his arms and hugged him. It was over, finally. She started to shake. Slade hugged her close to him. He never wanted to go through that again.

The Captain of the bomb squad came over to Catherine. "That was extremely smart, Catherine. You saved a lot of lives today. I can see by the blood in your ears that you need to go get looked at in the Emergency Room. Maybe Slade can force you to go, because I know you won't listen to me."

"I will go as soon as we get finished here, Captain." Catherine was surprised to feel Slade pick her up in his arms and head for the elevators. "We will be back after she is looked after, Captain, thanks."

"But I need to talk to the twins and Barb..."

"Yes, when we come back up, you can talk to them. There is a police officer with them in the family room. She will explain things to them."

"There will be a lot of paper work tomorrow." Catherine's mind was wandering trying to cope with the trauma she had just endured. She was so dizzy and couldn't hear very well, but being carried in Slade's arms was nice so she closed her eyes. That wasn't a good idea; it made her extremely nauseous.

"Can we get a doctor to look at Catherine?" Slade was at the trauma center.

"So, what do we have here?" asked the physician on duty.

"She was on the fourth floor just outside the isolation chamber when the bomb blew. She can't hear, she is dizzy and she has blood in her ears." Slade brought the doctor up-to-date.

"Bring her in here, Detective," commanded the doctor.

"Any other symptoms, Catherine? Can you hear me at all?"

Catherine by Evonne D. Haley

The doctor was looking in her ears. Then he focused on her eyes. "Are you dizzy now?"

"You sound like you are in a barrel, Doctor, and yes, I am dizzy, plus I have a bad headache; but I am fine. I need to get back upstairs." She tried to sit up on the exam table.

"No, young lady. You are staying here for a while until I say you can go. If you were going home to bed, I might let you go in a few hours; but since I know you will just go right back to work, you will stay here until I say you can go. You stay here with her, Detective, while I go set up some tests for her. Was anyone else hurt upstairs?"

"No, because of her quick thinking, a lot of people were saved today. I will stay here with her until you get back, but I have to get back up there."

"Ok, I will only be a few minutes."

"Slade, I am fine here alone. You can go up. I know you have a lot of work to do and reports to write."

367

Catherine by Evonne D. Haley

"Catherine, we will have a serious conversation when you are better. I said I will stay until the doc comes back and I will. Everything will still be there when I get up there." Slade leaned in and hugged her. He kissed her softly and said, "Please don't scare me like that again, honey. My heart stopped when I saw that bomb. It has also made me realize that we don't know what will happen from day to day, so I plan on enjoying every minute from now on. When this is all over, you and I are having a serious discussion about our future."

Slade was interrupted as the doc came back in the room.

"I am sending you down to x-ray and the phlebotomist will be taking some blood. We will go from there, Catherine, but you will be staying overnight, so resign yourself to that. Nurse Ferguson will be keeping an eye on you and I will be back in a while to check on you." He squeezed her hand before he left.

"Ok, let's get you into a gown, Catherine." Nurse Ferguson was efficient with a no-nonsense attitude.

"I will be back shortly, honey." Slade was torn between staying with her and doing his job upstairs.

"Don't worry, Detective. We know what she did today and she is a hero to us all. We will take very good care of her."

"Thank you, Nurse. Here is my number in case you want to contact me." Slade wrote his number on a slip of paper and passed it to her.

"I'll see you in a bit, Catherine." He kissed her lips. He started to stand up, stopped and kissed her again. She smiled. His eyes promised more, later.

"You have a caring man there, Catherine. Now let's get you into a gown."

Slade stepped off the elevator onto the fourth floor to what seemed to be chaos, but was really organized chaos. Everybody had a job and they were performing them efficiently; there were just so many of them. He stepped up to the crime scene recorder and signed in as he put on the booties and gloves required at a crime scene.

"I don't know how she got him to go in alone, but it saved her life and many others. How is she doing, Slade?" asked Director Blanchette as he came over to him.

"They are taking good care of her down in the trauma ward, Sir. She has some bleeding from her ears; hopefully, her hearing will return in full. She also has a bad headache, and they are making sure she has no head trauma. I am going back down in a bit." Slade was looking around the scene; he then focused on the isolation doors and the remains of what had once been a human being. "Will they even have enough material for the medical examiner?"

"They will have DNA and the residue from the bomb, but that is about it. Those blast doors did what they were made for; to keep contaminants from escaping. I never have determined why someone would fasten on a bomb and then blow themselves up taking as many casualties as they could."

"I don't know, Sir. Maybe it is because we have such different cultures. Ours gives us the freedom to grow to become what or who we want to be and the terrorist culture is like a cult; no individualism, simply become who or what you are brainwashed to believe you are. I think Sameer was conflicted, because he became obsessed with the money Ron stole from him. Let's be thankful he never found it for he could have done a lot of damage with that amount of money."

"Yes, you are right. I am going down to see Catherine before I go back to the office. There will be a lot of paper work to complete," he warned as he left.

Slade left that wing of the hospital to visit with Sarah and Kara.

"Hi, girls. How is your Mom doing?" he asked as he entered the family room.

Catherine by Evonne D. Haley

"She is doing better, sitting up and she even had some Jell-O. How is Catherine? Is she alright?" asked Sarah.

"She is doing well. They are taking some tests to be on the safe side. She has some hearing problems, which should go away, and a headache, which should also go away. How are you two doing?"

"Good, now that we can see Mom improving. They are letting us go in to see her for longer periods and she is able to talk to us, but she tires easily. Dr. Sinclair is pleased with her progress. Did Sameer actually detonate a bomb in the hospital?"

"Yes, and if Catharine wasn't such a smart lady, others would have been hurt." Slade told them as much as he could and reassured them it was over, finally.

Slade looked up as Chuck walked down the hall towards him. A second later Kara screamed and tried to hide behind Slade.

"What is wrong, Kara? It's ok; it's just my brother, Chuck." He was trying to reassure her as he tried to reach around and pull her into his arms.

Sarah, however, was a fighter and she barrelled into Chuck. She was not going to allow him or anyone else to hurt any of her family ever again.

Chuck tried to fend her off as he was speaking to her in a soothing voice, "I am not going to hurt you, Sarah. Calm down for a minute and I will explain everything to you. OK?"

"Yes, I would like to hear this, too, brother." Said Slade.

"I was working undercover trying to get information about Petrov and his dealings with Sameer. The girls know me as Geb." Explained Chuck.

"Oh, that's why you looked so familiar," said Kara. "You look a lot like Slade, except for the scar on your face."

"Yes, and that's why I ran with Petrov at the airport in New York. I couldn't have my cover blown. I was too close to getting the information I needed. So, are we friends now, girls?" Chuck asked as he slowly took his arms away from Sarah and looked at Kara.

"Yes, if Slade will vouch for you," Sarah responded.

"Tough crowd," laughed Chuck as Slade reassured them.

"What are you doing here?" Slade asked.

"Just wanted to make sure with my own eyes that you and Catherine were alright."

"Yes, Catherine is downstairs getting checked out in emergency. She has some hearing problems from the blast and a headache, but the doc says he is keeping her just to make sure that is all. Thanks for coming though," Slade smiled at him.

"How is your mom?" Chuck asked the twins.

"Better," responded Sarah. "Although she looks terrible, she is more alert and can talk to us now."

Catherine by Evonne D. Haley

"I am going in to see her for a few minutes and then you guys can go in, Ok? Want to come in with me Chuck?"

As he agreed to go in with his brother, the girls smiled at him. "Sorry for attacking you."

"That's ok. You sure pack a punch there, Sarah. I'm glad you're on our side."

"Thanks," she responded. "And Detective Slade, we are happy Catherine has you now. She is such a great person." Kara smiled as he left.

Slade spoke to the duty nurse and then they went in to see Barb.

"Hi, Barb. How are you feeling?" he asked as he stood at the end of her bed. She still looked like she had been run over by a train, but she was awake and alert. "This is my brother, Chuck Slade."

Barb barely muttered, "Hi."

Then she went on the offense. "Detective, is Catharine alright? Was anyone else hurt? Is Sameer dead? Is Peter alive?" Barb was frantic with worry. The nurses said no one else had been killed but that's all they could tell her.

"It's fine, Barb. Catherine is being looked after; just a few problems from the blast, her hearing is impaired and she has a bad headache. I am going back down in a few minutes to see the results of the tests they were doing when I came up here. The only other person hurt from the blast was Sameer and he is dead; this time for sure. Catherine saved a lot of people with her actions. Peter is in Surgical Intensive Care and will be for a few more days. He really should be dead from taking a bullet directly to the chest, but he is a fighter. The bullet hit him high in the chest and not near his heart or other organs. It was the information he gave us that saved you and many others at the Tower. He stayed conscious until he could tell me what was planned. The doctors still don't know how he had done that. I think it was you. He was so scared Sameer was going to kill you that he sabotaged his job of assassinating the

Ambassador to save you. That is in confidence. There is a lot of red tape and reports to get through, but Director Blanchette thinks we might be able to forgo his arrest, especially now that we know there was CIA involvement. We will see what happens. Now you just need to get better. Do you need anything?" Slade asked.

"Are my girls alright?"

"Your girls are great, Barb." Spoke up Chuck. "Smart and caring, like their mother I think."

"I am so appreciative of what you and Catherine have done for us all. Peter knew he could turn to you. He is not a bad man, Detective. He was co-opted into a place he didn't want to be in, but couldn't find his way out, until now. Thank you."

Slade could tell she was tiring; her voice was getting weaker and her breathing was faster.

"You are very welcome, Barb. Get some rest. The most important thing for you now is

377

to heal. I will tell the girls to give you a few minutes before they come in." He patted her hand and then left to go see his woman, the woman he planned to marry.

Chapter 41

(Three months later)

From her chair she watched the cruise liner make its way out of port to head for a new destination where the passengers would spend more tourist money before returning home to their jobs and the routine of their daily lives. The sun was beaming down on her, warming her skin as the ocean breeze kept her cooler than the temperature on the thermometer.

It must be around noon, but she had thrown away her watch the day she arrived. Juan, her houseboy offered her more coffee, which she happily accepted.

"Gracias, Juan. Would you please ask Cook to bring the menu for dinner, por favor?" It was not a question so much as a polite command.

"Si," he replied and left to do her bidding. She was a nice senora, very kind and generous. The staff were happy to have her as their patron.

Catherine by Evonne D. Haley

Her hacienda overlooked the Sea of Cortez. This was the third home she had purchased, all under assumed names. She had learned from Ron when she had seen how he set up shell companies. It was amazing what you could do with enough money, and she had plenty.

Every morning at ten she watched the whales breaching and blowing as they played around the boats that were there every day to feed them so the tourists got what they paid for, seeing whales in their natural habitat, as fake as it was or as real as it seemed.

Two young women in colorful sundresses came down the steps to the pool area where their mother was relaxing.

"Ola, Mother," they said in unison.

"Ola, girls. What do you have planned today?"

"We are going into town to shop. Is there anything you need or want us to pick up for you, Mom?" asked Kara.

380

Catherine by Evonne D. Haley

"No, I gave a list to Juan. He is going in shortly. You girls have a good time." They both came around her chair and kissed her on the cheek.

Barb shooed them off as the cook, Manuel, handed her the dinner menu.

"This all looks delicious," Barb smiled at him." Would you please tell Juan to pick up the wine for dinner, and anything else you need. Oh, and there will be just three for dinner at seven-thirty this evening." She passed him back the menu. "Gracious, Manuel." He smiled and left.

She leaned back in her chair, soaking up the sun, the beauty of the flowers and the sparkling, blue water of the Sea of Cortes. It's waves crashing on the beach below to a gentle rhythm that almost covered the sound of her cell phone, a prepaid burn phone that would not be used again after the next few minutes.

"Good morning, love."

"Good morning to you, too, Peter." She replied. "How did your meeting go?"

"It went very well. Catherine says 'Hi'. She is really a smart lady and such a good friend to you and the girls."

"I know. She has been great. We couldn't have done this without her. So, what did the CIA say?"

"They said 'See you and have a good life'." They couldn't say anything else with Catherine and Director Blanchette of the CSIS there. He was not happy that the CIA had been operating in Canada without his knowledge. He made it clear he would be monitoring their activity more closely. He also told them that CSIS was thankful for my help in taking down Sameer and his cells; and if anything happened to either of us, he would use all his power to bring charges from the Director of the CIA down to the agents involved. After that they said I had given them all the information they needed during my de-briefing and I was free to go wherever I wanted. Blanchette said it was too bad they hadn't found the rest of the money Ron had hidden; and probably never would, so the case will sit on someone's desk for a while and then will become a cold case."

"As I was leaving, Catherine asked that you stay in touch with her; let her know where you are, since I couldn't. She said you have her cell phone number. It's over, Barb. We are free. We have enough money to keep us in a grand lifestyle for the rest of our lives. I can't wait to see you."

Barb smiled. "Me, too. Peter, before you go to the airport, would you please go to the apartment? I left my little ceramic pig on the desk and I don't want it to go to goodwill. It means a lot to me because it was a gift from Catherine and the girls."

"Da, no problem. I still have my key. I will call from the airport as we agreed and you can give the pilot our destination then."

Barb was a very intelligent woman. She had told her girls they were all in Witness Protection and could never contact anyone from their old life again, not even Catherine, Maggie or Ella nor any of their kids. It would not only put them in danger but their friends as well. Her girls had gone through enough bad experiences with Sameer that they would obey their mother without question. Barb was taking no chances that someone out there in Sameer's world would try to find them. No one could know where they were.

Peter didn't even know where they were. They had communicated only a few times on the burn phone. Barb said she had thought it was best for him to get his debriefing with the CIA finished first. That had gone smoother than he thought it would thanks to Catherine and Director Blanchette. Now, they could have a good life together, clear of intrigue and chaos.

Chapter 42

Catherine quietly entered the apartment with her spare key. She had just received an anonymous phone call telling her that the rest of the money Delong had stolen was at Barb's apartment on the thirtieth floor of her building. Something had been nagging at her sub-conscience and it was now screaming at her. She had to prove it wrong. Why didn't Peter know where Barb was? She had left the hospital one week after the attack and disappeared with her daughters. Then Catherine found out there was no insurance money. Did Barb run because she was afraid of the people who controlled Sameer, as Peter said she was? Or did she have the money? Why then did Peter not know where she was?

When Catherine entered the apartment, all seemed quiet. She became aware of Peter at the same time as he saw her.

"Hello, Catherine." Peter greeted her smiling as he came into the living room from the study. "Barb forgot her little ceramic pig.

She said it has great sentimental value as it was a gift from you, Maggie and Ella. It looks rather ugly to me, but I guess it is the thought that counts. It sounds like it has coins in it," Petrov said as he shook it. "Were you looking for something?"

"No, I just came to check the apartment one last time as the movers are coming tomorrow morning to take everything to goodwill as Barb requested. Maggie is listing it the day after tomorrow." Catherine said as she moved behind the couch closer to the door. She was holding her gun down by her side. She should have brought Slade or backup.

"Where is she, Peter? Is that a safety deposit key in the pig? That was a smart move putting it in Barb's apartment or did Barb know all along?"

"No. I didn't ..." Peter stopped and looked down at the little piggy bank in his hand. That was just too ironic, he thought. He realized he had made a monumental error in judgement. Barb had deceived him, played him like a professional. Now here he stood with the evidence in his hands. He couldn't even be angry, because he admired her. There were probably just enough gems in the pig to indict him as a co-conspirator for the theft of the millions Ron had stolen. He slowly moved the pig to his left hand; and as he dropped the pig on the floor breaking it open, he drew his gun with his right hand and held it down by his side. Diamonds, rubies and other gems spilled out onto the floor. He would go to jail for a long time. All his dreams had just smashed to pieces on the floor in front of him; no place in the sun, no millions to live on, no freedom, and no Barb.

Both Petrov and Catherine stared at the bounty at their feet; and then as their eyes met, Catherine brought up her gun and she fired.

As Catherine waited for her team to come to the crime scene, she wondered why she hadn't seen it before. Barb had been abused for over twenty years, lots of time to plan for her revenge and escape. Or maybe, it just fell in her lap. Catherine didn't hate Barb, but she did feel regret that she hadn't talked to her more and been there more for her. Maybe she could have convinced her to stop before she went beyond the point that she couldn't come back from.

Barb had set Peter up and Catherine did blame her for that, because Catherine now had that stain on her soul even though Peter had not given her a choice.   He had protected Barb to his last breath. The horrible thing was that Barb knew he would and that was the line that she should never have crossed. She used him. More, she used Catherine to kill him. She would someday have to account for her actions. But most of all, Catherine just felt so sad. Her friend was lost to her.

****

Although she had everything she ever thought she wanted, her freedom, no one to dictate her life, and no one to use her for their own goals, Barb knew she would miss her friends, and maybe, even Peter. But she also knew the freedom she now had was what she craved most; no, more than craved. Her freedom was vital to her survival. She had been smothered, trapped in a life that wasn't what she had wanted or dreamed of for so long. And it had all changed in an instant.

She couldn't figure out why Ron had taken Max out that pivotal night, until she noticed the different collar on her. It was almost the same but not quite. The clasp was different; it had three rows of diamonds instead of two rows of sequins. When she took it off Max, she felt more gems inside as well. It was all there, give or take a million.

It was at that moment she made a life altering decision to take it all, the money, the freedom, the life; she had it right in her hands.

Now she finally had control of her life, she thought, as she watched Max chase a butterfly across the lawn, the diamonds in her collar sparkling in the sun.

Catherine by Evonne D. Haley

Catherine was the first story in a trilogy of three women, friends who have supported each other through husbands, careers, kids, disasters, and celebrations of life. I hope you enjoyed *Catherine*. Her and Slade's story continues in the second novel, called *Maggie*, who sees a murder in one of the properties she is selling. Can Catherine and Slade get the killer before he gets Maggie? And can Chuck protect her until then? But then who will protect her from Chuck? Or does she want to be protected from him?

Maggie will be available in 2018.

Evonne Haley